Simultaneous Times

Vol.2

Simultaneous Times
Vol.2

SPACE COWBOY BOOKS

SPACE COWBOY BOOKS
61871 Twentynine Palms Hwy
Joshua Tree, CA 92252
www.spacecowboybooks.com

Simultaneous Times Anthology Vol. 2
ISBN #978-1-7328257-4-1

First Edition | 2021
Book design by Jon Christopher
Cover art by Zara Kand

CONTENTS

The Fiery Wings of Sleeping Birds

Julie Carpenter

Illustrations

Reagan Louise Wilson

<hr>

The wave of revulsion hit so hard that time stood still. The food on her tongue turned to ash, the breath in her lungs hot misery. Sidney's hand, poised mid-scoop over the cereal bowl, contracted into a helpless claw as the spoon clattered to the floor. Just when the weight of the air became intolerable and threatened to suffocate her, the world resumed speed and the sensations fled. She caught her wife's startled expression across the breakfast table and tried to signal that everything was fine, but instead slid helplessly out of her chair as her consciousness failed.

She awoke to Freya's moon-shaped face hovering placidly above, a perfect satellite of concern.

"Syd, how many times is this now?"

"I... don't know, 5 or 6, how long... how long was I out?"

Freya sat down on the floor next to their overstuffed couch where she had arranged Syd's thin body in a nest of pillows.

"Long enough. Let's get you into Dr. Petersen for a scan—you can ride with me. I need to go into the lab to check on the latest implants anyway."

Weighing a protest, Syd finally shrugged and agreed to go. It had happened ten times, each time harder to shake.

Dr. Petersen's neuroimaging lab was on the floor just above Freya's department. Officially she was head of the Avian Comparative Molecular Neuroscience Laboratory, but the researchers just

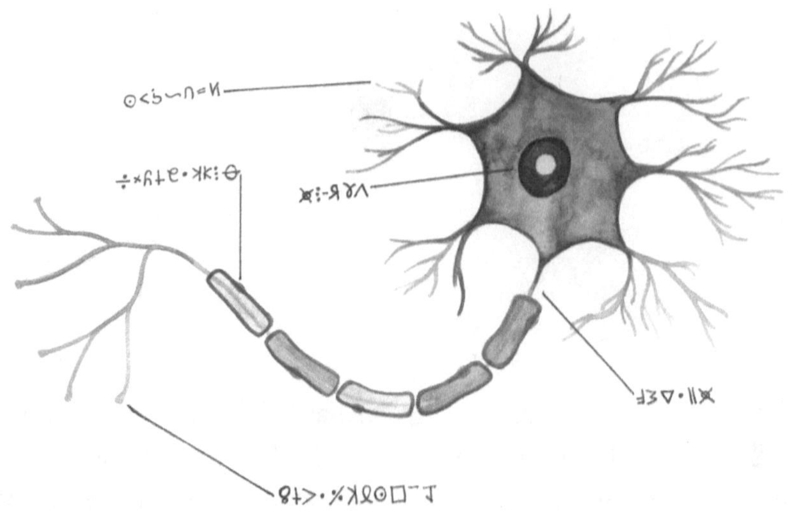

called it Ravenlab. She parted from Syd in the elevator and went to see the results of the latest experiments. When aliens first made contact fifty years ago, it became apparent that while the two species could communicate very simple concepts through great effort, any meaningful technical exchange was impossible. The underlying logic of the alien language was the outcome of their unique evolution, which while convergent with Homo sapiens in many useful ways was unimaginably divergent in others. For instance, in half a century of study it was still not apparent what the aliens called themselves. Their movements and motivations remained as inscrutable as the ancient gods of myth. They came and went from half a dozen landing sites around the world. Neither aggressive nor benevolent, they left an area when attacked and never returned to it. When approached, they allowed humans to examine them but often would suddenly terminate the exchange in a flurry of limbs and a torrent of otherworldly sound. Whether it was language, a song, or a warning was unclear. It was clear that their technology was so advanced as to appear magical. And facing an accelerating global ecological collapse, the human race desperately needed some magic.

A cacophony of croaks, clicks and caws greeted Freya as the lab door slid open. Ravens had been chosen early on as study animals because of their unique intelligence and linguistic abilities. Ten birds comprised the latest cohort. Freya and her colleagues had painstakingly rewired tiny regions of the ravens' brains to mimic patterns of neurons in the aliens' cognitive organs. Not the grand pattern, of course... that was the madness that Syd and Dr. Petersen pursued upstairs. Freya took a more basic approach. She hoped that by studying the leaf, she could understand the tree.

She donned a pair of gloves and opened a cage door, gently removing a glossy, black dead bird. Its back was broken, snapped as if a massive seizure had stiffened every muscle. For now the other birds survived, but it was likely only a matter of time before the same incompatible code killed them. It made sense. The aliens could break and reform their unusual skeletal structures easily, so movement at the expense of bone was not inhibited. This raven had broken his back by stretching his muscles past the breaking point of his spine. This group of birds was the 10th generation of birds bred from the most promising early alien to avian implant subjects. In other trials, some birds drowned in air when they forgot how to breathe, others refused to eat and starved unless force fed. The successful subjects could be roughly divided into Dancers, Speakers and Sleepers. The Dancers adopted erratic, stylized movements and odd spatial orientation, often hanging upside down. Speakers chattered away in what sounded like the alien speech, but without syntax, much like a human baby babbles phonemes before learning their parent language. Sleepers, well, they slept... they took food if offered but remained permanently asleep in one hemisphere of their brains according to scans. Some neural implants led to birds that fit the categories neatly, while other combinations led to birds with a mixture of these traits. One nerve cluster at a time, Freya was identifying which patterns could be assimilated by terrestrial organisms, and which were so foreign to life here as to be fatal. Freya took a seat at her computer to share the results with her team.

On the floor above, Syd awaited the results of her scan. After removing the Medusa's tangle of electrodes from Syd's shaved head, the doctor took only a few moments to deliver the verdict.

"Incompatible. The alien neural clusters are threatening her basic brain functions" said Dr. Petersen, glancing away from Syd trembling on the edge of the cot and towards his three young interns and the glowering military liaison. He turned back to Syd, and added gently, "But we knew that, didn't we?"

Her elfin chin dropped slightly. It wasn't fair, she'd come so far and they were tantalizingly close to a breakthrough. Syd was both an exobiologist and an epileptic, a unique candidate for Petersen's program. As a child, her brain had been surgically divided to ease the electrical storms that crippled her. Now, like one of Freya's birds, she had received grafts of the alien brain patterns. But unlike the ravens, her divided mind kept her human self safe in her left lobe while they slowly implanted the alien operating system on the right.

Gradually, through drawings, dreams and hypnotic sessions, precious fragments of alien intelligence began to filter out through Syd. She felt so close to understanding something fundamental about them, but it eluded her. And apparently would elude her forever, as the alien patterns were now jumping the gap and wreaking havoc. At any moment, they could unseat her mind and leave her a vacant shell. That, or her heart could beat so fast that it exploded, or so slowly that she would simply slip away. She was less afraid of death and more angry at her helplessness. Perhaps it was a symptom and not an inspiration, but Syd desperately wished to continue. She decided to ask to test one last hypothesis. Petersen

ran his hand over his own scarred, bald forehead and agreed that, given the situation, the risk was acceptable.

The bell at the lab door startled Freya out of her analysis. Petersen's intern Michel was standing outside the shatterproof glass, looking like he'd been sent to his execution. She buzzed him in and he handed her a folded paper. Her world teetered a bit on its axis as she read:

Dearest Freya,

By the time you read this, I will be asleep. In my dreams, the lucid dreams like we practiced, I will be able to find out who they are, why they are here. And what they have that could save us, and how to ask them for it. I have told the doctor to graft to me everything we have, but if I was awake it would destroy me. So he must induce sleep and dream state. Do you remember when we met you said, "We have no gifts from the gods, only the gifts we give each other?" Well, my gifts to the world are these scars in my head. I hope that your gift will be to find a way to heal them and wake me up safely. It's like when I got stuck in the mud driving into town during the floods, and you were so furious but you came to save me anyway. You said then that your birds were smarter than me, and it's true… at least they didn't volunteer for this. I've asked Petersen to turn over all of his data to you and to make you a full partner in the project. I'm sorry, there was no time and if I saw you again I never could have done it. I'm sorry I didn't tell you how far we had gone. Please wake me soon so I can grow my hair out long again, like when we were young.

Your foolish bird,
Syd

From the Angels
to Snakes

Susan Rukeyser

Illustrations

Zara Kand

K aylee was born on December 31st, 1999, a day expected to end with mass computer failure and societal collapse. When nothing happened, her mom told her, it seemed the future was saved.

Today was Kaylee's fiftieth birthday. Like every day, she was shocked awake at 5:00 a.m. Bright fluorescents clicked on, and Adam, the virtual assistant now required in every American home, announced: "Welcome to another workday!" Mandatory wake-up lighting was part of 2031's Traditional Morality Initiative, or TMI.

Kaylee slid her journal from its hidden spot beneath her bed. She wrote, "You desire men." It was all she could remember from last night's Non-Male Bonus Retraining, or NMBR. She knew she risked imprisonment, writing anything. She stole a glance at what she'd written the last few mornings: "Childcare is the noblest profession;" "Angry women are ugly women;" "You are satisfied."

President Jedediah Winthrop, known as Father Win, took office following Trump's triumphant second term. Trump departed the White House in his new TiltCOPter, flashing cameras with a final thumbs-up and, with his other hand, a raised middle finger.

Father Win's Traditional Values party soon controlled all three branches of government and eliminated term limits. Father Win currently enjoyed his fifth term with little doubt of a sixth. A beefy evangelist from rural Georgia, his campaign slogan was: Purity Above Pride.

"Forgetting something, Kaylee?" Adam's voice boomed through her apartment—just one room, because, like all Workers, she was poor. Kaylee pinched the cartilage just above her left earlobe, initiating her auditory implant's Daily Underachiever's Motivation—Female, or DUM-F: "Good morning, ladies! Let's see your best smile. Work hard today to nurture the next generation of Real Americans™."

The recording ended and Kaylee lowered her feet to the cold white floor. *Fifty* years old. When she hit age forty-five without successfully producing children, Kaylee was notified that her Citizen's Classification had changed from Breeder (Potential) to Breeder (Failed), and, because she took a Gender Studies course back in college, she was added to the Misandrist Activity Watch List, known as MAWL.

At UCLA, she was a music major. She fell in love with her cello's deep, smoky tones, everything it expressed between her knees. Now, all women worked in childcare. There was no music.

"I'm up!" she called, waving at Adam's camera. She looked down at her stubbly legs. Kaylee knew she'd be ticketed, if a man saw her like this. Women weren't allowed to see each other's legs, beneath their required tunics.

She walked to the kitchenette, where her ration of pre-mixed "coffee" dispensed. Kaylee ignored her rumbling belly. She had to conserve her rations until next week's paycheck. She filled a water bottle from the tap and added a purification tablet. She was thirsty but the pill needed time to work.

Kaylee pulled a heavy coat over her tunic, since temperatures in Los Angeles—renamed The Angels after 2039's sweeping American Language Act—hovered around freezing since the partial climate collapse. She fastened her respirator mask and tied her boots for the two-hour walking commute from the former Koreatown (now known, like so many places, as MAGAville) to the daycare center she was assigned to in Beverly Hills. The sky was its usual yellow-grey. When was the last time she saw a bird? she wondered. Or any animal.

On Wilshire Boulevard, she fell in line with her fellow Workers. No one had cars anymore. The wealthiest Job Creators drove ex-military vehicles. Throughout The Angels, roads were broken by earthquakes and sunken by floods. Kaylee heard rumors that, east of The Angels, in the Mojave, the skies remained blue. She'd hiked there as a child. Kaylee remembered her mother's face, lit by joy as she posed atop piles of rocks.

The only sound, aside from shuffling boots and the occasional light armored vehicle, was the spillover from the ads playing on everyone's implants. The ads were synced automatically with the digital billboards along Wilshire: designer respiration masks, ex-military Float Boots, fertility-enhancing gummies, over-the-counter Ciproxicillin (or Roxy, as it was known), the latest broad-spectrum antibiotic to treat everything from Typhoid to Syphilis to the Salmonella poisoning that most people learned to live with, these days. Kaylee couldn't afford any of it. Only Billionaires stayed home and shopped.

Kaylee thought: It's my birthday—is it so wrong to want a present? Maybe a chrome-handled Suck Pen, she thought, pulling out her cheap, plastic one. Women needed to sweeten up, Father Win declared at his inauguration. Suck Pens delivered glucose and fructose with an estrogen-progesterone infusion. The increased oral cancer risk was dismissed as irrelevant—who didn't have cancer, now? At tax time, women submitted proof they'd bought enough.

Tonight, like every night, she would fall asleep immediately, exhausted by hours of walking and tending to other people's children. She would not receive a chrome-handled Suck Pen or any present. No one knew it was her birthday; her mother was long dead. Happy fucking New Year, Kaylee whispered, so Adam wouldn't hear.

The next morning, Kaylee woke, rolled over, and wrote: "Enough."

The morning after that: "Stop."

Kaylee was concerned. Her NMBR must be malfunctioning. She skimmed her recent entries and, no question—there had been an abrupt, recent shift.

The following day, she wrote: "Desert." She stared at it on the page, trying to remember how it was pronounced in the NMBR transmission: "desert," like the Mojave? Or "desert," as in leave and never return? She hid the journal and pinched her ear: "Good morning, ladies! Let's see your best smile."

About an hour into her walk down Wilshire, she approached

the abandoned tar pits, still bubbling their ancient stink. She turned when she heard a light armored vehicle behind them. It was high off the ground, each wheel on its own extended axle. It plowed down the middle of the road, hitting several Workers.

"STOP!" Kaylee hollered, and the vehicle skidded to a halt.

A white man in an expensive respirator mask jumped down from it. "Got something to say, old bitch?"

Kaylee froze. He strode toward her and punched her hard, just beneath her ribcage. She dropped, the wind knocked from her. Her fellow Workers did not stop. They did not even slow their pace but stepped around her. The white man yanked off Kaylee's mask, cutting her nose. Acrid air stung her throat. "Breathe deep," he spat into his fancy mask. He flashed what had come to be known as The Billionaire: a simultaneous thumbs up and middle finger.

A young Breeder (Potential) stepped over Kaylee, the hem of her tunic lifting to reveal hairless ankles. The man grabbed her and dragged her from the road, down onto the sandy ground near pools of tar. No one interfered.

Kaylee was banged up. She knew without looking that a bruise bloomed across her torso. The man was on the girl and everyone walked past. The billboard ads continued: "Why spend your life on the toilet? Try Roxy today!"

"ENOUGH!" Kaylee yelled. The man looked up, and she knew: she might not survive this. She strapped her mask back on and stood on shaky legs. She limped to the far side of the man's vehicle and leaned against it to catch her breath. Then she realized—he'd left the engine running.

"Desert," she remembered. "Des*ert*." She climbed into the vehicle and looked at the controls. It was an older model, electric. The battery charge light was green.

She pinched her ear to silence the ads. She knew a report would be issued and her Adam would be patched in: "Kaylee, you seem upset. Come home, I'll draw you a bath." If she ignored him for too long, he'd forward her coordinates to the police. From up here, she saw the suicides swinging from lampposts outside the former LA County Museum of Art.

She began a U-turn, careful not to hit any Workers. The seat gripped her thighs and the vehicle announced: "Female, perimenopausal. Sober. Underweight. Pulse and respiration rapid due to stress. Have you tried ChillZout, from Compliance, a Traditional Values, Inc., company? Your first dose is free!"

The man finally noticed Kaylee stealing his vehicle and ran into the street, clutching his unzipped fly. He screamed, "How *dare* you, Worker?"

She wanted to run him down, smear him across Wilshire Boulevard, reduce him to the nothing he'd made of that girl. She wanted his corpse left to rot while Workers stepped over him. But she steered away, bound for the Mojave. She needed blue sky. She needed to know it still existed. She sent an apology, unheard as a prayer, to the girl lying on the ground, as if the man still held her down.

By the time she passed the empty strip malls of Riverside County, her whole body ached, and she was furious. Her fellow Workers were cowards. She was a coward. Why did they fear death, when this was life? She was done hiding. She pinched her ear, and Adam resumed immediately: "Kaylee, you seem upset. Come home, I'll draw you a bath." An ad followed, synced with a billboard: "Yummy Mummy Gummies, just 199 dollars a day!"

She entered a twisty pass, and both Adam and the billboards fell to static, then silence. The road disintegrated and the vehicle said: "Self-navigation initiated. High-travel suspension engaged. Take your hands off the wheel."

Nearing Mount San Jacinto—known as Mount Saint Hyacinth since the American Language Act—she saw the lake that now filled the valley. Propellers from antique wind turbines littered its shores.

Through her implant, she heard an unfamiliar, female voice: "33 9248 N, as in November. I repeat…33 9248 November."

Was she a cop? Kaylee wondered. Is this how I die?

The woman's voice returned: "115 9294 W as in Whiskey…that's 115 9294 Whiskey…do you copy?"

"Hello?" said Kaylee.

"Answer 'Yes' when your vehicle asks if you want to follow those coordinates. See you soon," the woman added, signing off.

Adam crackled back to life: "Kaylee, you seem—" but then the vehicle entered a steep grade, and Adam was lost. The vehicle asked if she wanted to follow the coordinates and she said yes.

She saw signs for the town of Joshua Tree, long since evacuated. There were no roads there anymore. Each of the vehicle's wheels tackled the rocky terrain independently. The billboards remained, although here the videos sputtered, and the audio was out of sync. The vehicle proceeded slowly, going almost vertical at times as it traversed rocky hills and sunken washes. Where were the Joshua Trees? Kaylee wondered. The yucca, the mesquite?

The vehicle turned into the decommissioned National Park, passing a dilapidated ranger station. Inside the park, the billboards were dark and silent. The vehicle followed what remained of the main road, past lakes that formed when the desert flooded. The sky was indeed blue here, and Kaylee cried from the beauty. She removed her respirator mask, because if this air would kill her—so be it.

The vehicle signaled that her destination was just ahead. Kaylee saw an expanse of cholla, barbed spines gleaming gold in the afternoon sun. Beyond them was nothing but flat, open desert, the wind whipping sand across it, and in the distance: piles of rocks, tall as mountains. She saw a few parked vehicles but no people.

Kaylee called, "Hello?"

"Hi," answered the voice from her ear. A woman stood right in

front of her, beautiful and old, with wild hair that matched her silver jumpsuit. She pointed to her scarred left ear. "I'm deaf in this one, so talk to the other." She started down a washed-out trail and soon struck out through the cholla. "Watch yourself," she warned. Kaylee drew her arms close to her body, but barbs snagged her tunic. She couldn't return to The Angels like this.

When they were through the cholla, the woman hiked across open desert. Kaylee struggled to keep up, her scraped knees singing with pain.

"I'm Nan," said the woman. She stopped and pointed at a lone, rangy bush. "Creosote. They used to be everywhere." Nan resumed walking and it seemed she was headed for the nearest mountain of rocks. The rocks were smooth and piled on one another like scoops of half-melted ice-cream. Kaylee felt a stab of hunger. In the afternoon's lengthening shadows, Kaylee saw in the rocks the shapes of ravens, coyote, and the most intimate parts of the human female.

When they finally reached the rocks, the sun was low and red. Nan led her around to the far side, which couldn't be seen from the road. Kaylee heard the rattlesnakes first, then the women: her age and older, chatting and laughing in folding chairs, stirring soup and chili on campfires, while the snakes shook their warning.

"Knock it off, kids," called Nan, and the snakes quieted. The women all wore the same silver jumpsuits. All had bloody bandages against their left ears. Kaylee didn't see one Suck Pen.

Kaylee said, "I thought maybe you had a spaceship out here."

Nan threw back her head and laughed in a way that made Kaylee want to light her up like that again. "No, honey, we're human. Was it the jumpsuits? We just think they're fun, like the cool sci-fi future we imagined. You got better questions than that?"

"What is this place?"

"A singular, electromagnetic aberration. We extract our implants and the Adams can't find us. Women can just be, here. Or they can go home."

"I don't want to go back to The Angels."

"I meant home, as in what's through there." She pointed to a fissured rock in the far formation, just enough room for an under-weight body to squeeze through. "We hack the Adams of Failed Breeders. We've all been there. When we saw you transcribing your NMBR transmissions, we knew you were one of us. Don't worry—we blocked Adam's view."

Kaylee whispered, "Are you misandrists?"

Nan chuckled. "Sometimes," she said. "But, listen—we don't want a revolution, just peace and quiet." She saw Kaylee eyeing the cleft in the far rock. "Why don't you check it out, after you get some food and first aid?"

"Are you coming?"

"I stay here," Nan said.

Kaylee was disappointed, but she was determined to go. Soon, her belly full and wounds dressed, Kaylee looked toward the far formation. She caught a glimpse of a woman atop the rocks, lit by joy. Kaylee trudged to the crevice and tried to peer through. Was that music? An unaccompanied cello suite—Bach. She re-membered it from college, when she held love between her knees and wrote without fear and believed the future would be better. Seized with longing, she turned sideways and started through the cleft. She looked back once, for a glimpse of blue sky, but by then it was already dark.

Jim Daring
and the Return of the
Sky-Lords of Venus

Jon Christopher

Illustrations

Rik Verlin Livingston

———●———

"Jim Daring grabbed onto the pole and swung down to the next level while firing with his atomic blaster. The Sky-Lords popped in and out of existence to avoid Jim's deadly accurate blaster fire. Blam, Blam, Blam! The Sky-Lords couldn't move fast enough and several of them were splattered across the spaceship hull. The rest of the Sky-Lords fled into the Time-Void.

"Quickly, Jim untied Maya who was lashed to the nuclear bomb in the center of the Venusian spaceship and pushed a button on his power-belt that activated the trans-materialization device. In seconds the two were standing on the deck of The Invincible, Jim Daring's trusty spaceship."

Larry Stewart paused a moment, "and that's all I have so far. It's really rough."

"But I want there to be more Venusian spaceships." The voice on the other end of the line was Rick Schneider, A.K.A the famous author G.S. DuPont. "They should be large ones built in the cloud cities of Venus in the year 3153."

"What's your plan for these spaceships, and why the year 3153?" Larry was making notes as he listened to Rick Schneider, a successful real estate agent, who had hired Larry to ghostwrite the last seven books in his "Jim Daring, Galactic Hero" series. The series was a big hit with the young adult market. The books were put out like clockwork every six months, under the pen name G.S.

DuPont. The next one in the series, the one Larry was trying to write, was called *Jim Daring and the Return of the Sky-Lords of Venus*.

"The Sky-Lords come from the year 3153, don't you remember? And I want to have the spaceships attack the Earth, or an Earth Outpost in orbit around the moon, call it Spacelandia." Once again Rick was changing the story line on Larry.

"And any special weapons this time?"

"Yeah, Atomic Time-Disrupters and Nuclear Beetle Bombs."

"Nuclear Beetle Bombs?"

"Small nuclear bombs, smart bombs that gather into clusters and multiply their explosive power. They can cover a spaceship in a matter of minutes and then, boom!"

"Nice, which side has the Beetle Bombs?"

"Neither. The bombs self-replicate and attack anything that moves. They live in swarms in space. That's gonna be the twist for the ending that leads to the next book."

"Really?"

"Yeah, just make it believable sounding."

There was nothing believable about a Jim Daring story. It was based on the successful formula of action and more action that Larry followed for every story with a few extra details thrown in to keep the stories fresh. Jim Daring was a handsome bachelor and genius inventor who regularly saved the planet from certain destruction, horrible space monsters and the evil Dr. Kraft.

Jim had blonde hair and blue eyes, stood six foot one and a half inches tall and had an IQ of over 200. He had a muscular frame that made Maya, his "almost-girlfriend", swoon whenever Jim would take off his shirt. In every book they would, invariably, go swimming in Jim's Olympic-size swimming pool on his private island, or his private yacht, or personal spaceship. And in every book there would be a moment when it looked like Jim and Maya might fall in love, finally, but something would always happen and

ZONO ART
Galactic
HERO

they would continue on as "just" friends. Apparently this ongoing theme was really driving the sales of the book among the demographic of girls, age eleven to thirteen.

The last few Jim Daring books hadn't sold as well as *Jim Daring and the Sky-Lords of Venus* had when it came out two years ago. Those had been pretty exciting times as *Sky-Lords* moved up the sales charts to end up as the third bestselling young adult science fiction book of the year. A major movie studio optioned the book. Larry had been signed to ghostwrite the next five books in the series. Now, with sales lagging, this next book really needed to be a "big win for the team" Rick Schneider had told Larry.

Larry, as the writer, was the lowest paid member of the team. Ellen St. Marie, the illustrator of the whole series made more than Larry. Rick Schneider, of course, took a much larger chunk of the money because he's the one who actually had the contract with the publishing company and owned the rights to the name G.S. Dupont. Rick had never actually written a whole story, but he was a fountain of ideas.

Larry was the fourth ghostwriter on the series which had been going on for fifteen years and included twenty-five books. The first writer had completely disappeared without a trace and the second writer had died mysteriously after writing the wildly popular *Jim Daring and the Caves of Medusa*. The third writer had a heart attack. The team jokingly referred to the situation with the ghostwriters as "the curse of Jim Daring", Larry didn't find the idea very amusing.

As a professional writer, and a single guy with no one to please but himself, Larry centered his life around his work. When he was in the midst of a book he ignored his phone, for the most part, except when Rick called. He had to answer when Rick called nearly every morning with new ideas for the current book, which often required long hours of re-writing. As frustrating as it was to ghostwrite for Rick, Larry really enjoyed the challenge, and the plot twists Rick would come up with on a regular basis were usually far-fetched and amusing.

Now, it was Thursday afternoon. Rick had called and said he was flying to Switzerland on business. This sounded strange to Larry, but he didn't question it because this would mean days of writing without Rick's input. Last month Rick had traveled to Iceland on business and was gone for over a week. It had been glorious.

The day was proceeding splendidly. Larry had gone to the store to stocked up on supplies, frozen pizzas, frozen burritos, frozen mac 'n cheese, and beer, lots of beer, and was prepared to hunker down and write. After several hours of writing he was starting to find the pace of the story. He had a few new ideas, a few scenarios he thought he'd try out. He had his word processor humming a quick pace as his fingers flew over the keyboard.

All the Jim Daring stories began when Jim was interrupted in his lab, or in a meeting, or during a TV interview, with important news that needed his immediate attention. Jim's butler, Manfred Smits, was usually the one interrupting Jim.

"Manfred, can't you see I'm busy?"

"Sorry sir, it's the President – it's urgent."

And so the latest terrible news would be delivered. Sometimes it was a threat of monsters or asteroids from outer space, sometimes it was a volcanic eruption, or tsunami, or a typhoon of cosmic proportions, and sometimes it was Jim Daring's nemesis, the evil Dr. Kraft.

Jim would swing into action with blaster firing, inventing new weapons to deal with the latest threat. The solutions to the stories often bordered on outlandish and ridiculous, but somehow, over the course of the story it all seemed plausible. In a wildly popular story, *Jim Daring and the Sky-Lords of Venus,* Jim had invented an atomic blaster which would send the Sky-Lords into the Time-Void, where they would be imprisoned forever. Now, for this sequel, Rick had decided that the Sky-Lords could come and go as they pleased from the Time-Void, creating a huge plot hole in the story. It was these challenges, and the fact he had two more stories to go on his contract, that kept Larry writing. Sometimes it kept Larry drinking.

Larry worked on the story late into the night, slept for a while with the story buzzing in his head, and got right back to it as soon as he had coffee. There was no one to interrupt the flow and after a microwaved burrito he was ready to write until… whatever came next.

It was getting near dusk when Larry heard an urgent knock at his front door. He tried to ignore it, but someone called out his name.

Larry was astonished when he opened the front door. "I know you!" He was face to face with Jim Daring, and he looked exactly like Larry had just written about in the story. Jim was wearing the same shirt with horizontal red stripes, his blue skin tight pants and black space boots.

"Oh course you do, everyone knows me. Quick we have to hurry!" and with that Jim pulled Larry out the front door and started to push him towards the front walk.

"Hold on…" Larry started to protest.

"No time. The Sky-Lords have returned and we have to go, NOW!"

Jim Daring's rocket ship was a short distance away. Larry could see a figure waving at them. As they got closer he could see it was Maya urging them to hurry. She looked prettier than he had imagined. Larry climbed as quickly as he could up the ladder into the rocket ship with Jim right behind him. The instant they were belted into their seats the rocket shot off into space.

Larry was breathing heavy. He wasn't in the best of shape and that had been quite an exertion. While Larry tried to catch his breath alarms started to go off in the rocket ship.

"Incoming," shouted Maya.

There were bright flashes out one of the view windows.

"Atomic missiles destroyed," reported Maya.

In five minutes the rocket ship was docking at a giant spaceship. Larry recognized the ship from his own writing.

"Welcome to The Invincible," said Jim, expansively, waving his arm like a showroom model.

"Yes…" Larry was truly amazed to find himself stepping onto the deck of The Invincible. The spaceship was solid, even more so than he had imagined. His shoes hit the metal deck with a soft thud. He noticed details he hadn't imagined, like the battle-blaster gun mounts on every wall. And the fire extinguishers. He never described fire extinguishers in any of the Jim Daring books.

After what seemed like a brief five minutes of peace and quiet an explosion rocked The Invincible. The lights went out for a moment and red emergency lights came on.

"It's the Sky-Lords. Direct hit by an Atomic Time Disrupter. We're reeling in the years," yelled Maya, pointing at the ship's chronometer.

"Activate the temporal-stabilizers!" shouted Jim. Maya punched a button and everything went black. Time slowed down to a crawl. With immense effort Jim slowly felt his way to the chronometer. He had only seconds, but seconds were like hours, and it seemed like days before he reached the chronometer and inputted new time coordinates. The ship shook and blinked in and out of existence several times. It heaved with an ear-splitting sound and then everything was quiet. The lights soon flickered back on. Larry, Maya and Jim were all collapsed on the floor.

In the amount of time it would have taken for a short commercial break the three started to come to their senses.

The new time coordinates had been entered wrong, and now The Invincible was in the year 3153, and the solar system had changed. The clouds that obscured Venus had been driven away by Earthlings using powerful Cloud Driving technology. The planet had been transformed into a bustling world of Neo-Earthling colonialism and commerce.

The Earth itself had changed in many ways. The formation of The United States of Earth in the twenty-first century had led to nearly five-hundred years of uninterrupted progress, until the surface of the planet had been completely remade in man's image. There were several bands of sky-ways that circumnavigated the planet, which housed massive cities 200 miles above the planet. The sky-ways were tethered to the Earth with giant gravity lift elevators. Above the sky-ways, orbiting the planet, were the seven Cities of the Masters, including Spacelandia, the seventh and newest of the cities.

Terra City was one of the oldest elite cities high on the edge of space. It was known as the place of old money. No one was allowed to visit Terra City, ever. Among the other cities were: New Earth City, Gaia City, New London, New Washington, New Moscow, and of course, Spacelandia.

The Invincible docked at Spacelandia, the home and domain of Alex Von Werner IV. With approximately five square miles of building space, the city was fantastic beyond anything that had been imagined up to that point. The shape of the city was constantly changing and used quantum spacing to house the hundred thousand individuals that made up the city. Quantum spacing was a new process that allowed for space and time to be warped on an individual basis to make sure no one ever invaded your personal space. On the commercial level it allowed for multiple condos to be built into the same space. Even though there was theoretically no limit to the number of condos that could be built in one space, building code insisted on a limit of ten.

Once on board Spacelandia, Jim, Maya and Larry were escorted to luxurious suites to refresh. Soon the three were gathered around the Olympic-size swimming pool with a view of North America out the space viewing-windows. Jim took off his shirt and jumped in the pool, Maya felt a little flush as her pulse quickened at the sight of Jim's manly chest. Larry felt a little embarrassed and pretended to stare out the view-window at the planet below. He was rather confused by the recent turn of events and was trying to figure out how he had gotten into a Jim Daring story.

This little moment of relaxation was interrupted by the arrival of the Sky-Lords in their fleet of large Venusian spaceships. The Sky-Lords were lighter-than-air jellyfish-like creatures over ten feet in diameter with long, dangling tentacles. Once, the Sky-Lords had ruled over the vast cloud cities of Venus. But the cloud cities had all been destroyed during the previous book, and now, in the year 3153, the Cloud Drivers had made the planet uninhabitable for the Sky-Lords. As soon as the Sky-Lords escaped from the Time-Void they headed straight to Earth to exact their revenge on Jim Daring and the inhabitants of the planet.

The Sky-Lords attacked Spacelandia first and were quickly able to board the city on one of the flight decks. One of the Sky-Lords jammed several tentacles into the metal flooring of the flight deck and the whole city began to shine with a menacing purple glow. Jim Daring jumped from the pool, threw on his shirt, grabbed a blaster and took off running towards the flight deck. While Jim ran he invented a new weapon, an Atomic Time-Neutralizer, by grabbing various objects he saw lying around as he raced through the corridors. Maya and Larry followed after Jim, struggling to keep up.

Jim Daring arrived at the flight deck and happened to be only a dozen yards from the Sky-Lord with its tentacles jammed in the flooring. He blasted it with the new Atomic Time-Neutralizer. The Time-Neutralizer worked like a charm and vaporized the Sky-Lord instantly and forever.

SKY-
Lord
ZONO
ART

"Take that you slime bucket," yelled Jim. Maya arrived and stood with her back to Jim, blaster raised, firing at the remaining Sky-Lords who kept popping in and out of existence.

In moments Jim had vaporized every Sky-Lord on the flight deck who hadn't escaped back to the Time-Void, with his new weapon. Then Jim blasted the entrance to the Time-Void with the Atomic Time-Neutralizer and sealed it for all eternity. Maya and Jim hugged and almost kissed, but Jim's wrist-watch two-way communicator buzzed – it was the President calling to thank Jim for saving the Earth!

Larry, who had been watching Jim Daring's heroic deeds from a few yards away felt something snap in his brain and his mind did a little glitch. Things went black for a moment and then there was a brilliant flash of light. He felt himself pulled into some kind of a light tunnel and he disappeared.

In a minute Larry found himself back home, answering a frantic knock at the front door. It was Jim Daring again, beckoning Larry to join him to save the planet from its latest menace, the Nuclear Beetle Bombs. Without a pause Larry rushed out of the house to join Jim and Maya on their rocket ship, racing off into their next adventure to save the Earth again.

This is when Larry Stewart went missing and didn't return Rick's calls anymore. It seem to everyone involved as if he just vanished into the twilight. A week later police detectives came poking around, asking questions. Several neighbors told the detectives that on the evening he had disappeared Larry had run from his house, yelling something about the Lord, something like "The Lord is coming". No trace of Larry was ever found, in spite of the substantial reward posted by Rick Schneider. Rick, of course, hired a new ghostwriter to continue the series. No one on the team has mentioned the curse to the new writer.

The
Activator

Anastasia Wasko

Illustrations

Zara Kand

ONE

The Activator's first sonic movement in centuries went unheard by Machine sensors. But the scream displaced the tiny Earth-satellite's electromagnetic waves. The motion of the material of the magneto-sphere caused the dry, dusty floating rock to rotate thirty degrees towards the sun. The surface dust grains (red—white—brown—black, soft turquoise green and darker soft turquoise green and fuzzy white) illuminate.

A hand-forearm poking through the surface of the tiny Earth-satellite, the hand-forearm that had felt cold for years, sensed warmth. The ice around the protrusion started to thaw in the solar rays, exposing more arm, arm hair, gray-frozen skin, fatty porous material, blackened fingernails.

The trans-man inside (underneath) is alive.

The woman inside (underneath) is alive.

The Activator is divine kind. It watched when the woman cried, scratched, and clawed at air as she was chained in during the preparation. The Activator watched as the woman watched her love, also saddled in chains, screamed. The Activator screams again, making the waves of space-time grate against each other. The tiny Earth-satellite rotates further. The ice layer melts more. The ice is becoming softer. The fulgurite casing is starting to fall apart.

Quantum science had established four Earth centuries ago that the soul-to-incarnation vessel process in the end-time of the current yuga was unstable. Transition pending.

But Souls were incompletely incarnating. The humans discovered this by measuring the spirit mass of babies. Quantum science data fed the Machine government, and it outlawed this dysfunction; it was called the ether-mass precision law. Machines dictated that no gender dysphoric Bodies be permitted to enter the next yuga. If the baby wasn't killed at birth, it was inquisitional through childhood and adulthood. Shots were administered in the vaccination programs. Adulthood extermination came by vagabonds disclosing their whereabouts inadvertently, because those not in a comm don't care what the information does to the person of suspect. They talk freely. Gossip. You just need to listen to everything around you.

The Machines are living systems. They were created by humans to sustain infrastructure that sustained Earth habitability, and eventually humans let Machines create most living environments. Machines know best what we need to survive, thought the humans. They are self-regulating, thought the humans. But this is how Machine AI infiltrated the biorhythms of Earth Mother (a feat made possible after humans held her captive through their rampant misuse of her biorhythms, anyway). So, humans also allowed space imprisonment: Machines knew best. Consciousness, perpetuity, inaction. A block in the birth cycle. That was the punishment for being on Earth. They estimated when too much bio-mass was accumulating; they estimated what Earth Mother could sustain. Earth's Machine governments launched captured undesirable humans (chronicled in the Incomplete Incarnates Inquisition, those with a gender dysphoria) to space in gypsum capsules, blasted with Earth sentiment and catapulted into space to be a prisoner in asteroid orbit. A human was chained into a gypsum capsule so the heat of propulsion would be endured. The body needed to remain intact (to not induce human death and soul-detachment-from-body and forward the reincarnation cycle).

Earth Mother was becoming Hell through practices.

The Activator had sounded.

And Machines could not fathom divine intervention.

Transition was upon the yuga, and the Machines were meant to stay in the hell they created.

The two prisoners in their fulgurite asteroid, their tiny Earth satellite, were where they awoke to the presence of the Activator. It bites the rock with skeleton teeth, throws pebbles to the side. Dust stirs. The side of her body that contains organic skin (flesh-covered hand, wrist, arm, rib cavity, breast, nipple) slide over the smooth gypsum crystal; she touches the rock. She tries to move her body. It straightens then slumps. Her head bows sharply to the side—bears her dusty teeth. Empty eye sockets look toward former lover. Years of entrapment on the fulgurite-asteroid decimated their physical forms, but not their souls. She knew the form of her lover. She reaches again to her lover despite her lover's distance. Grit slides from her forehead into sockets.

"Why are you eating the dirt!" he screamed.

"It," she corrected.

"Whatever the fuck it is, why!" he screamed again. He couldn't move his body, only pieces of his lips, and his eyes. He was helpless to move his legs and torso. He had awoken in strange Space to see a light hovering over his woman, and then the woman awoke with a fervor and zeal that matched only her hatred for the Machines. Now he watched her, the creature, eating. The bone side of her body that is skeletal (exposed hand, wrist, arm, rib cavity) hangs loose, buoyed by light gravitational force on the fulgurite asteroid.

They had fallen in love. But the Machines had deemed him an undesirable, an Incomplete Incarnate, even though the fact was false. Machines could not discern the qualitative differences in human souls; they only measured quantitative differences. Machines don't care. When the trans-man's lover wouldn't leave his side, she was imprisoned and cast out, too.

Activator placed the node of a vivaxis on the woman's skull forehead. Connection. The light beam went through the woman's skull. Hole in the skull. The force of the Activator's press of the sun turned the asteroid.

The sun broke the woman's body. She tumbled into space and became entrapped in the atmosphere.

And then she fell to Earth. She fell in pieces. She rained down, seeds of space and alien environments and vastness: seeds in the Earth.

The soul that was in the body of trans-man, imprinted into the grains of the fulgurite asteroid that now dispersed through space, watched Earth: a rainbow exploded from the impact of collision: Mother Earth to Mother Seed.

TWO

Most of her fell into Joshua Tree, a scorched desert and former stargate on Earth.

The human body—the carrier for the Activator—ruptured into tiny parts, into seeds, into bits of interstellar dust, into droplets of air and material, into a tiny concept of a thing as it (collectively, the pieces) rode down to Earth concealed by atmosphere-dust-ash smoke ignited by the friction fire of descent. The pieces reconnected on Earth surface, moved by subtle vibrations, catalyzed by the slow and thick blasts of mysterious objects. The blasts altered the telluric current of the grid around Joshua Tree, which allowed Earth energy to prevail over AI networks. (Grid consistency never happened and the military base [operating Machine sensors], source of the blasts, never figured it out.) The Earth wanted to receive the Activator.

It took days to assemble herself and days to acclimate to the body that was her carrier. The quantum composition of the body was not changed; the Activator powered it as the body's soul.

Whole body, able to process sight: she looked at the rocks. Soft, smooth red-mauve-salmon speckled with black and white quartz. Fulgurite existed here, but it was described "cat skat rock" because it looked like (on Earth) pieces of that timeless shape, cat shit. She heard the words come from a space inside the head. But she didn't know the meaning of cat, or cat skat rock. She didn't have the experience of cat or cat skat rock.

Power.

She needed life to life in the dust to dust of Transition.

She felt the ambient energy instinctively. Fulgurite held dead power. She needed live power and felt it coming from tall spikes planted by human hands. She started to walk along the high tension lines. At the poles, she climbed up. She took the cables in her hands, bit them, chewed on them. Before she slid down, she ripped out a line and sucked on it until the line went taut. She left it and walked on. The electricity put a sweet taste in her mouth. Satiated.

She walked. Far out into the Joshua Tree zone the telephone poles and power lines became fewer. The horizon showed formations of rocks with rounded edges, twisted trees with tufts of spike leaves, sky unobstructed for miles. She walked for turns of the sun: rising, setting, light, dark.

And then the Moon blossomed.

That dark cycle, the Activator felt the Moon in full power. The silver disk struck rays of the Sun from Moon's surface to Earth in a strength that galvanized karmic patterns embedded in the Activator's human body. Full Aries Moon. The Activator became a huntress, turned on a flight for safety, walking across the barren Earth field was no longer enough. She must kill that which makes her unsafe. This programming entered her (sub)consciousness field.

THREE

The space is empty of humans at the early light hour – she enters the mouth of the concrete street. Neon lights. 24-hours fast food and deli stops. Tall palm trees, barber shops, massage parlors, flags from the Empire of America line the road on which the Activator, Carolyn, feels the most concentrated power. This is the road she is called to walk.

She climbs up a telephone pole and snaps the wire attached to it. There is a shape—a metallic (network)comb—at the top of the pole, too, and she stares at it as she holds on to the pole drinking power. Her body starts to go numb. There is more in the power line than solely electricity. She spits out the tip of the wire and looks up. Faint waves of current create a ripple around the metallic (network)comb. She slaps the device and it falls off, whirring. A slow and thick (mysterious object) sounds.

[on the base] "A transmitter just went down," said the private squat encharged with monitoring the 5G network.

Sergeant staring over shoulder at screen of grid map. "Are the aliens arriving?" he asked.

Another voice, feminine, said, "No, sir. No scheduled meetings."

Sergeant puts hand on the gun in his belt holster. Unlatches safety. "If the aliens aren't arriving and their ship's throwing off the signal, I bet it's those goddamned townsfolk. Those goddamned townsfolk know they shouldn't mess with the towers." [/on the base]

Slowly, she slides down the pole. Sun is getting stronger now; humans start to emerge sitting in cars behind wheels. Carolyn takes extreme notice of all of them: human organisms with souls buried so deep under layers of control, manipulation, and conditioning. Tears form in her eyes. Her human-ness shows. Rivulets of purple blood start to quietly slide down her back.

The Activator remembers the previous Yuga; during Transitions between yugas, a power control erupts across the galaxy. Worlds that are dying plead for their continued existence. Worlds that can adapt, do. And worlds that have Change Agents send them across time and space so they can be planted as seeds. But, divine in nature, Change Agents like the Activator suffer from non-human-incarnation memory. Before the language (and associations) of the humans in the current yuga can be imbibed, the non-human memories must be laid in the carrier DNA in neat order so that it can be resuscitated when the divine spirit returns to an origin yuga.

All worlds and all yugas exist at the same time. Transitions happen when controlling sentience on a native planet become too powerful for its own good. The AI on Earth is at its tipping point.

So the Activator/Carolyn can never be seen for the being that truly is; humans call this pain. Divine call this prowess. Life on Earth means you are passed by everyday because no one acknowledges you. So Carolyn moves through 29 (a designation that only represents physical location in Earth terrain; named towns have stories, and this one doesn't; the military demands that) and is not seen by anyone. She is just beginning her hunt. This is how Earth allowed people to be sacrificed.

Earth wanted to return to reptilians, anyway.

A military police vehicle comes careening down the road. It stops next to the pole that she had just descended. A man in a uniform gets out, he stands over the fallen metallic (network)comb. He looks violently left and right. He looks directly at Carolyn, a short woman, nondescript, brown hair, clothed in baggy jeans and long sleeve shirt, nondescript. He looks past her. He puts his hand on his gun, draws it, and shoots the bum sitting on the corner across the street under the loud neon light-sign of the dollar store.

"The Machines say to leave the equipment alone. So leave the equipment alone!" he shouts, after he has shot the homeless man dead.

He never saw Carolyn. This triggers: Memories of resistance surface into the skull area: *this is not a world that should survive.* Memories of being divine: *you will never be seen for what you are.*

This is a reconnaissance mission, timed, fated, and only for those who are able to leave the humans who have been corrupted by subservience to the Machines behind. So Carolyn lets the Sergeant live, she takes the homeless man's soul, now standing by the piled, slumped, bloody, filthy body under the loud neon light-sign of the dollar store. She embraces the soul, and sends it to Paradise in interstellar space.

An Asteroid for All

———●———

Brent A. Harris

———●———

Illustrations

Zara Kand

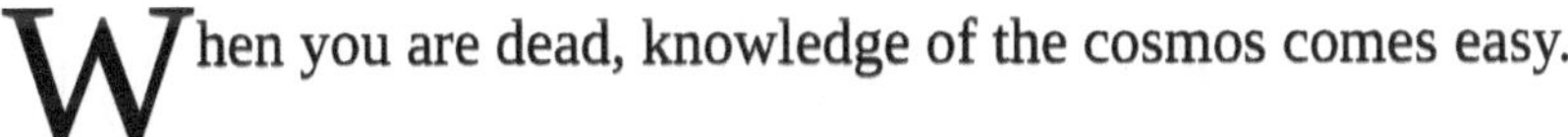

When you are dead, knowledge of the cosmos comes easy.

The gas giant beyond our asteroid had risen to its zenith, bathing white rock in soft luminescence unmarred by shadow. At this hour I take to walking. It is a time where I can gather my thoughts, breathe deep the thin air undetectable to most life in the galaxy, and lord over the creatures that crept and crawled under my leathery, clawed foot.

Our asteroid was large, large enough to have its own atmosphere and gravitational pull, but smaller than most moons, and of a size where we had carved out our dominance among the subspecies which dared to dwell with us. Where I walked was busy, but only with beings beneath me. I stepped where I wished, tolerating only the pink blooms of some flowering moonbushes lining the walk. I ignored the sickly-sweet smell of the flowers as I came upon a single black speck on the ground.

The speck was an ant-like creature, a *parvus*. They are scaly, small, with six legs, thick mandibles sturdy enough to carve through rock, and thick glassy eyes on stalks raised above its ugly round head. There were more of them on this asteroid than there were of us, but they were insignificant insects, and we were *imanis*.

I raised my clawed three-toed foot, scaled and toughened, and

gave no further thought to the creature as it crunched beneath me. It should have been the end of it. The creature was no winged warrior.

When I was a hatchling, my father had abandoned me, as was our custom. I was of the age where I understood the concept. I was to wander away, to forge my own path. He granted me the rite-of-passage name of Faliscan and bade me goodbye.

As he turned to trudge away, leaving me in a rock-strewn meadow of flower and abandonment, I failed my father. I ran after him, tears streaming wetly down my face. A loud wailing that I did not recognize as my own echoed along the empty valley as I chased after him. My clawed feet were not as tough as they are now, and I stumbled through a field of flowers.

I'm not sure if I stepped on that winged warrior's stinger, or if it attacked me, but if my father had not returned to fetch my purplish and swollen body and taken me to a healer, then I would have died as a child, even if my life, my failure, brought shame down on us all.

Back on the path, I raised my foot, and the creature that I had crushed came with it. Half its body was smeared on my claw. The other half was flailing, little legs kicking in the air, eyes swinging wildly atop their stalks, pinchers wide in what might have been a silent scream. I shrugged giant grey shoulders – as if they could feel pain anyway.

Nevertheless, I brought my foot back down to finish the job. The insect flattened, ground into the grooves of the ground, and I carried on.

Until I found another one.

It became like a game. The gas giant glowed softly. The flowered fragrance no longer cloyed my nose. I was bathed in a pure light. I found each *parvus*, asserted my dominance…

And stomped.

I continued along in this manner for what seemed an age. I came to yet another black speck on an otherwise spotless white walk and once more, raised my foot, a bent smile affixed to my skeletal visage.

And then my smile slipped off my face, the skin above my white eyes wrinkled in confusion, and I hunched down, nearly on all fours, so that I could better examine the microscopic miracle unfurling before me. The little black *parvus* raised itself up on its hind legs, as if it were standing in defiance.

In defiance of me.

That was not the natural order of things.

I should have pressed down, squelched my claws from side to

side and killed the creature quick. That would have stopped the game. But I was granted a curious mind, a vastly superior mind, one in which I was to lord over all, and this brave little bug intrigued me.

I kept my foot up in the air.

Another black insect skittered out from a hole in the rock toward the shadow of my foot.

And then another.

But this last *parvus* was red where the others were black. There were *parvi* aplenty out here under the deep pitch of sky and stars. They kept to themselves in their own holes and their own tribes and underneath the feet of our rule.

Except for these three who all stood there. In insolence.

I almost stepped on them just containing my chuckle.

More *parvi* poured over the walk. Red, brown, black.

Small. Big. Queens on milky wings. Some with only five legs. Others with bent backs. Many had terrifyingly large mandibles. Fewer held no discernable threats at all. Everywhere there were *parvi*.

Lower creatures.

All around.

They streamed out of holes and burrows until the walk was thick and dark, wriggling and writhing, and swirling underfoot.

I stood there, amused, until my lifted leg began to feel fatigued.

I could not hold my mirth or my foot any longer. I let it fall to the ground with a crunch. Even with our lightened gravity, the effect was deadly.

The creatures could not have felt a thing. Their deaths were swift. It was as if I had stepped on seashells along the shore on some watery world. It was a cracking, brittle feeling, followed by a soft, slimy soup as liquified innards oozed around my claws. So much death with so little effort. All of them, beneath me.

The sunlight shifted off our gas giant. Its light began to retract, as if sucked down the horizon as day broke into blackness.

I didn't notice the first insect crawl onto my foot. The walk was swarming with them, and the little bugs that I hadn't stomped into oblivion were now skittering, en masse, along my leg.

I gasped at the realization. They were on me.

I raised my leg once more, leaving a sucking sound as my foot pulled away from so many oozing carcasses, so that I could reach down to wipe away the invaders with long, bony fingers.

A pinch ripped into my leg. Sharp and painful. I winced just as another creature bit into thin flesh wrapped tightly around bone, until even their bites began to chip away at my skeletal-self.

Hurriedly, I brushed them away only to find several suddenly crawling onto my fingers, chomping and tearing at each one. I tried to hurl them off, but by then, there they were on my arm, my other leg. And the saggy, fleshy bits in the middle.

Everywhere, they pinched, everywhere, they ate, gnawing, tearing flesh, biting bone. Red welts dotted my skin, my arms flailed about, feet danced, my mouth closed and anus puckered, lest they crawl through other, more vulnerable areas – red parvi, black parvi, queens, fat ones, skinny ones, broken ones, and parvi in between.

Blind, I stumbled wildly, feet falling onto more of the wicked creatures. I sickened at the squelching sounds I made, no more, no more, no more…

My thigh caught against a thick branch of a moonbush. I lost my balance, and tumbled into it, pink petals exploded around me. And out from the flowers emerged a strange thing.

My fall had disturbed a winged warrior. A small, plump thing on thick, stumpy wings about the size of a stone and blue as a comet's tail. One side of the warrior's blue body held a sharp stinger, venomous and deadly to only the smallest percentage of us imanus. Its other side held large black eyes. Eyes which loomed over me. Angry eyes.

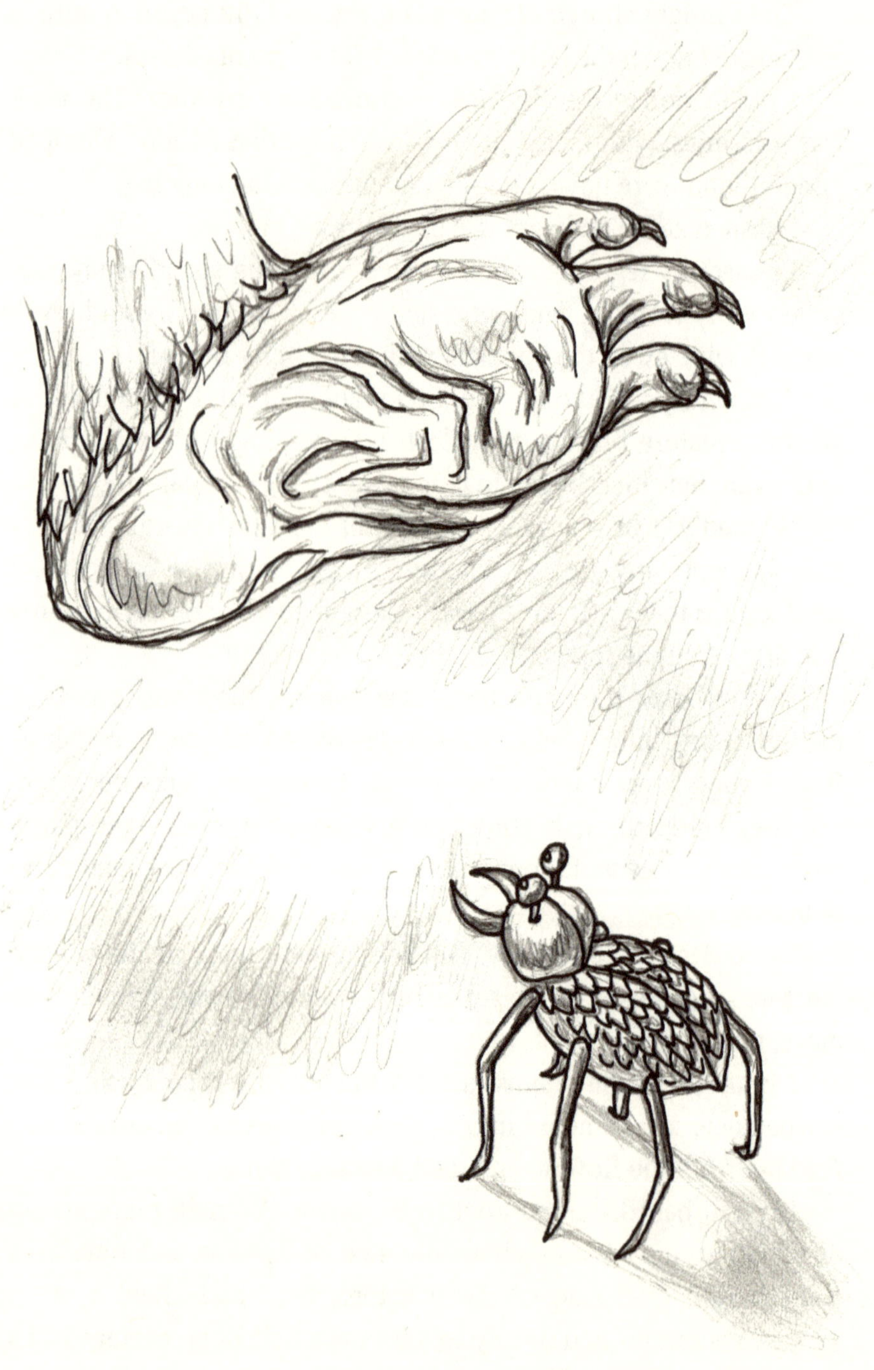

I am allergic to warrior stings.

Fatally so.

My father's face filled my mind. I was dragged back to the time in the field, when I was left alone, foot freshly stung. Dying.

This winged warrior, however, hovered at my face, darting left to right, right to left. I would have been fine, its anger would have eventually ebbed. It would have drifted away to some other pink petal.

But the bites and the welts and the pain from those *parvi…*

One tore into the fleshy bit between my thumb and finger. I screamed and swatted my hand away, shaking the creature off and infuriating the winged warrior even further.

It found my face.

The stinger stabbed at me. A web of pain shot through my left cheek. A soft, wet sponge of blood and guts trickled down my face as the warrior pulled its stinger out and died. It had given its life to take mine.

For the second time ever, I was afraid. My body was covered with creatures meant to be beneath me. My throat tightened. I could no longer fill my lungs with air though my eyes filled easily with tears. I wished for my father to carry me home once more.

I suppose, I could have gone around those black specks. I regret that now. There was more than enough asteroid for all.

Effigy

———●———

Jean-Paul L. Garnier

———●———

Illustrations

Jeremy Szuder

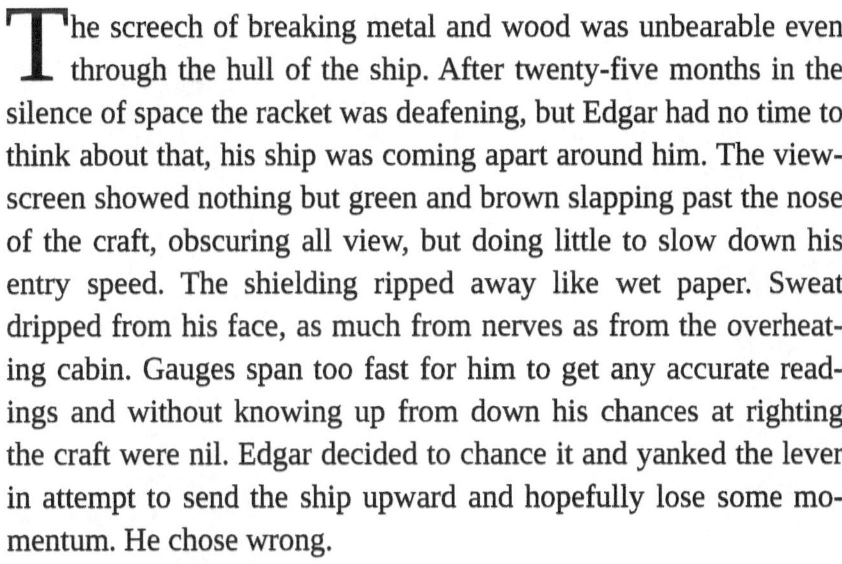

The screech of breaking metal and wood was unbearable even through the hull of the ship. After twenty-five months in the silence of space the racket was deafening, but Edgar had no time to think about that, his ship was coming apart around him. The viewscreen showed nothing but green and brown slapping past the nose of the craft, obscuring all view, but doing little to slow down his entry speed. The shielding ripped away like wet paper. Sweat dripped from his face, as much from nerves as from the overheating cabin. Gauges span too fast for him to get any accurate readings and without knowing up from down his chances at righting the craft were nil. Edgar decided to chance it and yanked the lever in attempt to send the ship upward and hopefully lose some momentum. He chose wrong.

Edgar awoke and assumed that the dampness around him was blood. He could see nothing through the eternal blackness. Crawling on all fours, looking with his hands, he discovered that the wet ground extended far beyond where he had regained consciousness. He ran his fingers over his body looking for injury, and surprisingly, found that he was intact. Nothing broken, no flesh torn. But this did nothing to stop the pain, the throb in his head, or the dry harshness of his throat. He fumbled through the darkness until he came into contact with the ravaged nose cone of his ship. Its injuries far outnumbered his, but it was something familiar in the

EDGAR.F

blackness. Searching with his arms outstretched he realized that this section of the ship was the only remnant in the vicinity. He dragged himself inside the torn opening of the cone and curled in a ball waiting for sleep, while noises from unknown life yanked him back to cold black reality repeatedly.

Suns rose one after another until the jungle lit up with every shade of green, yellow, and a few colors which Edgar could not recognize. There was only visibility in the direction in which his craft had parted and snapped the trees. He struggled to his feet and surveyed what was left of his ship. The areas of the craft that contained his supplies were nowhere to be seen, probably somewhere far off towards his entry point. *I must have hit at too steep an angle, the atmosphere seems thick. This isn't what the readings from Star-Base predicted. They won't even know I'm in trouble unless I can locate the radio, and my supplies could be hundreds of miles off for all I know.* Edgar shook these thoughts from his mind and inventoried what was left inside the nose cone. As he entered a cry from the distance sounded, he froze trying to identify it, but nothing in his mind matched the beastly terror that had billowed out of the jungle. He told himself that he had imagined it and went back to his work. The cone contained next to nothing. His heart sank, all that was left was a plasma cutter, wall mounted and virtually useless to him. It was stored there for ship repairs and parts fabrication, but there would be no repairs, there wasn't even a ship left.

Edgar fell to his knees in despair. A plasma cutter and a nose cone were hardly what he needed if he were going to survive. Another shriek emerged from the jungle and kicked his survival instincts into overdrive. He needed a weapon, or at least something to fend off whatever demon lurked out there in the trees. Then it struck him like a meteor. He reached for the plasma cutter and furiously began hacking at the remains of his ship until he had removed the basic shape of a scimitar. He beat it flat with two rocks then wrapped the crude handle with a vine pulled from a nearby tree. He held the simple sword in his hands and raised it to the sky. Pointing it toward the three suns he yelled, "I will survive!"

His cry vanished into the trees and a moment later was echoed by another more ominous. His brief hope shrank. *I must move. Find a way out of this tree cover, see where I am.* He scanned the surrounding landscape, then took off running in the direction of the felled trees, hoping to find something of his ship and supplies. Hoping to find anything that might help him survive this unknown wilderness.

He ran for hours, driving himself towards exhaustion. Mile after mile the jungle remained the same. Downed trees, twisted vines, and the horrible howling that seemed to surround him. Nearing the point of collapse he tried to push on, then heard a new sound penetrate through the trees. Water. The soft gurgling diverted his attention as he cautiously left the path that his ship had carved. Moving slowly he came upon a clearing. A gentle brook sparkled and flowed before him. Edgar fell to the water and gorged himself, forgetting all foreign dangers and lingering in the sweet relief of something cool to drink. As he lay sating his thirst a crash rang out through the clearing. He rolled over, sword in hand. Before he could see the creature it was upon him, dead from a bleeding hole pierced through its belly.

The beast was heavy and it took all of his strength to roll the carcass off of him. *I was lucky this time. I better watch my back.* The animal was huge. Armored like a rhino, but clearly with the agility of a cat. Edgar stared at its six legs and marveled at what speeds such an animal could run. Had his sword not struck its stomach it would be him that was lying there dead. Yet his hunger led him away from these thoughts as he set about the ugly work of ripping into the thing's flesh and building a fire to cook the foul smelling meat. It made him wretch, but if he were to survive, he must eat.

Edgar had no way of knowing how long the days lasted. The disorientation of the three suns and the jungle filled horizon left him no way of understanding the length of the days. But the length of the nights stretched out before him in an endless nightmare filled with the sounds of strange beasts and foreign winds. Having no agenda other than to survive he followed the path carved by his crash, hoping all along that the stream that had sustained him roughly followed the same land.

He was able to sustain himself by snaring smaller prey during the brief time he spent sleeping, and the random fruit found hanging from branches, unpalatable but edible. Day after day this scenario repeated itself until he had counted twenty-four success-ive nights where all three stars dipped below the horizon. On the twenty-fifth rising of the small suns, he felt weary and was yet to find any remnant of his craft. The scimitar was heavy in his hands. The tightness of his calves matched only by that of his thighs. Still, he ran on.

Somewhere in between the noons, he saw a glint in the dis-tance. This first change in scenery spurred him on with newfound vigor. He found new speed, yet paced himself knowing that this change could be a lifesaver. When he arrived at the obstruction in the landscape he found that it was only a shed piece of the hull. Nothing else was present, but the area had been cleared of branches and a great circle of stones had been erected around the debris. Not far off in the distance Edgar could see another piece of the craft shining, thoroughly unwelcome and foreign to the rest of the terrain. *It must be a much larger section of the craft. Perhaps now my hopes are warranted.*

When he reached this section of the ship he found that it too had been cleared of debris. Again a large circle of stones, this one even grander. He froze in position. This site added to his hope the feeling of being surveilled. Hands had done this work and it gave him the sense of foreboding that accompanies all men under attack. But the attack didn't come. He surveyed the jungle in all directions and saw no movement. Assured that he was alone he entered the torn section of his ship. It was a hollow shell, if anything had remained it had been removed by the makers of the stone circles. Disheartened, but grateful for a familiar shelter, he lit a small fire and curled up to sleep, keeping the scimitar in hand as he drowsed off into dreams of shrieking jungles.

Edgar awoke to a sizzling sound. The fire had been doused and steam rose from the extinct flames. Before moving he surveyed the scene. There was no mistaking that someone or something had thrown water on his fire. Intense cold surrounded him. He saw nothing in the darkness. Then a face appeared to him through the pitch black. Before the face a crystal on the end of a staff glowed a faint purple. A hand extended, pointing at the remains of the fire. Unintelligible words were spoken, but it sounded as if they were addressed to someone other than him. The staff reached towards the fire pit and reignited the fire as if by some kind of magic. In the light Edgar could see that he was surrounded by three women wearing loose gowns, all of the same color. Again the hand pointed to the fire, and this time, in the light he could see that the head was shaking back and forth with the universal gesture for 'no'. Then the flames were doused again and all was black. Silence spilled over the scene as he was irresistibly pulled into a deep sleep.

As he came to again he felt around for his scimitar. It was missing. So were the women who had stood over him the night before. Now it was day and two of the suns were already high in the sky. All traces of his fire had been removed, even the ashes. He stood and surveyed the scene. The stone circle around the debris was immaculately constructed, as if the builders had started working the moment the craft had crashed and not ceased their toiling until a level of perfection had been attained. *Why would they put so much care into building this? And they didn't harm me in anyway, just put my fire out. What could their motivation possibly be?* The women left no trace that they had even visited the scene, save for the circle. And they had left him alone. Again he searched for the scimitar. Nothing except the hollowed piece of hull remained in the vicinity. Without much hope he continued in the direction he had been headed. If he were lucky they hadn't gutted every section of the craft. Unarmed and frightful he sulked through the felled trees. There was no longer any need to run, he knew he was being watched, he could sense them everywhere in the jungle.

The howls from the jungle continued endlessly. When they rose to a fever pitch he broke a branch from a nearby tree and stripped it of its leaves to form a crude club. Without the sword he was vulnerable prey. *I doubt those women would help me if I were attacked again.* A rustling in the closest bushes peaked Edgar's senses and without thinking he ran towards the sound, beating the shrubs and vines with his club, making as much noise as possible. The jungle fell silent except for a few cries from far off birds. He yelled as loud as he could, attempting to exert his dominance over the landscape. Then a deep silence grew from the trees followed by an echoing of his shouts. Screams came from everywhere around him, growing into a chorus of fear. But it was his fear that grew. The cries from the jungle sounded as if they were a mockery, or was it veneration?

Terror struck inside Edgar's heart which pounded like a hammer on an anvil. His sauntering was over and again he broke into a rapid stride, trying to cover as much ground as he could. Trying to distance himself from the horrible shrieking. How long he ran he could not say but one of the suns was setting when he found he could run no longer. He kneeled panting, gasping in the heavy air. When he caught his breath he looked up at the path. In the dying light of the last two suns he saw a glint that looked as if it were coming from metal.

As he approached the glare he crossed another large circle of stones. Within this great circle was another formation made from rocks. From several yards away he could see that the stones were laid out in the shape of a giant scimitar. Within this imitation of his sword, precisely in the center, he saw his weapon sticking out of the ground. It was the source of the glare that had drawn his curiosity. Again he broke into a run, defying his aching muscles. Reaching the sword he drew it from the ground with some difficulty. The metal was warm as if someone had been holding it for a long time. Sword in hand he sensed the hairs on his neck begin to rise as a wave of anxiety overtook him. Someone was nearby. He could feel their eyes on him. How many he could not say but he knew that he was probably surrounded.

He fled from the clearing and plunged into the tree cover with wild abandon. From now on he would not loosen his grip on the scimitar, his only tool, his only chance of survival. He could hear branches snapping all around. Someone, many people, were crashing through the trees behind him. Fatigue was burning in his limbs but he could not risk capture, if that is what his pursuers had in mind. For all he knew it could be much worse than that, perhaps they were hunting their next meal. But they had left him sleeping before. Why had they not taken him then if that is what they wanted? So far he had seen no trace of anything manmade save for the debris from his ship. Where were they coming from?

Edgar ran on, and on, slashing vines out of his way with the handmade sword. He could not tell how long he ran but when he finally stopped to catch his breath the jungle was silent. No sounds of animals or people. Complete silence. The jungle was now shrouded in darkness and he had no way of telling which direction he had come from. But he had to make his way back to the channel carved by his craft. The ship and its precious supplies were his only hope. In this total darkness he would not be finding his way. He would have to wait until the suns rose again to get his bearings. Incredible thirst made itself known and he wished that he had consciously followed the creek instead of bolting off aimlessly.

Slowly he groped his way through the trees hoping to catch the scent of water. Judging by the broken branches in his wake he picked the direction that he thought led back to the clearing, proceeding with caution. With any luck he could make his way back to the stream undetected. Every few steps he stopped to listen to the jungle. Silence. He wished he still had the energy to run, but even if he did it could be futile with no way of knowing if he was headed in the right direction. Fatigue began to overwhelm him once again. Finding a sheltered nook beneath a giant tree he curled up to try and get some rest. Fearing that his sword might be stolen again he ripped a vine from the nearby branches and tied the weapon to his hand. He tugged on the sword several times, making sure that it was secure, then drifted off toward dreams of better times.

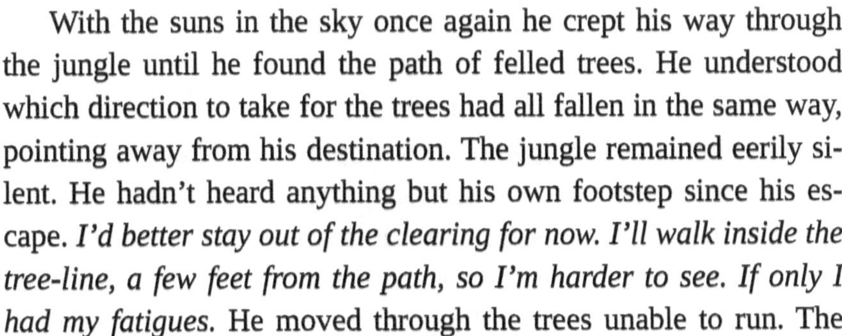

With the suns in the sky once again he crept his way through the jungle until he found the path of felled trees. He understood which direction to take for the trees had all fallen in the same way, pointing away from his destination. The jungle remained eerily silent. He hadn't heard anything but his own footstep since his escape. *I'd better stay out of the clearing for now. I'll walk inside the tree-line, a few feet from the path, so I'm harder to see. If only I had my fatigues.* He moved through the trees unable to run. The shrubs and vines were too thick for a quick pace. Edgar could feel eyes on him from every direction but saw no one, no animals of any kind. The silence continued. Sensing a presence but hearing and seeing nothing made him fearful.

Walking through most of the day he saw nothing. No signs of his ship, just endless jungle. But he had to go on. The silence was merciless. It filled him with hopeless loneliness. He tried crying out to see if there would be any response. None. Dread set in. Then panic. Forgetting all about his plan to stay in the tree cover he dashed out into the clearing. The jungle remained frozen as he broke into a run once again. Dizziness came on in waves as he tried to maintain his gait. He ran until he collapsed. The trees span. His senses faded back slowly. He was looking up at the last of the day's suns.

He drank from the stream until a semi-clarity returned. He sat rubbing his sore legs, longing for home, or the comfort of his spacecraft. He knew that none of these things were possible without locating the ship's radio. This knowledge alone kept him from surrendering to an unthinkable fate. Once again, he rose and started for the path. In the dimming light of the last sun he saw it. A large section of the craft, more intact than the ones he had thus far encountered. His heart surged. Maybe there was hope yet. With what was left of his energy he began to run again, slowly at first, picking up speed the closer he got to the wreck.

As he neared the ship he saw that it too had a massive circle of stones surrounding it. This circle was different than the others, it had been built up into a small wall. Clearly more time and effort had gone into the veneration of this section of the craft. The scene looked religious. He came upon the ship and saw that while it was largely intact, like the other sections it had been gutted. Then his mouth fell open as he gazed at what lay beyond the wreckage. It didn't seem possible but there it stood in front of him. He moved closer in disbelief. After circling the ship it came into full view. A replica of his spaceship, an almost perfect rendition, life-size and unreal in the fading light. It was nearly identical both in proportion and in detail. How the creators of the sculpture knew what the craft looked like before it broke apart was impossible to ascertain. Yet there it was, made of branches and vines. Edgar could see through the "window" that there was even an effigy of him piloting the ship. Fear gripped his heart. He looked around but still saw nothing, heard nothing.

He moved around the reconstruction slowly, taking it in from all angles. It was huge and must have taken many people with great skill days to construct. Why would they do this? And the sword outline made from stones. *Do they think I'm a God or...* Before he could finish the thought he came to the rear side of the sculpture. A large rectangle of boulders had been erected near the cargo doors of the facsimile. Within the rectangle was the body of the beast he had slain and eaten. What was left of the body had been laid out in a sanctimonious manner. He had killed the beast many days earlier but no signs of putrefaction showed on the animal's carcass. Considering how long it had been dead it was in pristine condition. And something else was wrong. There was no smell. The air should have been rank with decay but there was no smell at all. Only then did he realize that he had smelled nothing for days. The jungle was devoid of almost all sensory stimuli.

The silence broke. All around him the sounds of the jungle returned. Cries, shrieks from bird, leaves rustling, water gurgling. It was as if a mute switch had been turned off. With the sound came the smells: moist soil, vegetation, water, life. But still the body of the beast gave off no scent. It appeared serene, as if it were merely sleeping. Its face had a placid demeanor as if it was unaware of being dead. As if it had not died in combat. Something about the creature didn't seem right other than its lack of smell. *Why would such a foul beast be treated with such reverence? It's as if it meant something special to these people, whoever they are.*

As if this thought was a cue women approached from all angles, closing in around him in a massive circle. They all wore identical robes and advanced with slow, deliberate movements. An almost imperceptible hum came from the women. Its low tone was soothing but held ominous undertones. Edgar looked back at the creature lying within the stones. It looked even more alive now. It looked as though it awaited the approach of the women, as if they were intrinsically connected somehow. He thought he saw the creature stir. *But it's been dead for days. I ate him, he cannot be alive.* He knew that the beast could not be living, its flesh had sustained him. He had butchered it himself. Yet, as the robed women approached his fear of the beast was ignited. He almost expected the creature to lunge at him once more.

The hum from the women grew louder as they neared him, closing the circle. It was starting to sound like chanting. He could not make out any discernable words but they flowed from the women as though from a single mouth, perfectly in unison. Every other woman in the advancing line stopped as if it were previously choreographed. Those who did not stop continued closer towards him. He gripped the scimitar with all his might. *If they wanted to take me out they already would have. Am I really considering doing battle with these women?* He felt foolish brandishing the sword as if he were a warrior. He didn't want to put up a fight but his survival instincts had kicked in full gear and adrenaline pumped through his being.

The second circle stopped about fifteen feet from where he stood. Their chanting continued. One woman continued to advance. He recognized her from the staff she held. It was the same woman that had warned him about his fire. The look on her face, which was illuminated by the glowing crystal on her staff, shone grave and serious. She alone did not chant but the volume of the others increased as she neared his position. Her eyes stared into his soul. They were free from expression but their intensity made him nervous. When she was but feet from him she uttered a few unrecognizable words. He could not be sure if they were directed towards him or to the women in the circles. She raised the staff into the air as if to strike. He held his stance, not wanting to provoke a fight. Again she spoke the same words then pointed the glowing crystal in his direction. The crystal looked as though it contained lightning. After pointing at him she again raised the staff and this time pointed at the corpse of the felled beast. The crystal glowed even brighter now. Its lightning became more like the sun.

Edgar's heart pounded inside his chest. He was unsure how to proceed, or if he should attempt to communicate. *Maybe I have just stumbled into some kind of religious service. Maybe I should just back away slowly.* He took one step backwards then thought better of it. She had clearly been addressing him with the staff, it was no coincidence. *Maybe they are thanking me for slaying the beast.* But the look on her face was not one of gratitude. The chanting grew louder still. The lone woman walked up to the beast where it lay amongst the stones. She faced the creature silently for a long time. When she turned back to Edgar the look on her face was one of anguish and mourning. *Oh, no! This animal must have meant something to them.* Again she muttered unintelligible words. The language was guttural and strange, almost beastly.

She came towards Edgar. The pained looked on her face remained frozen. It was clearly directed at him. He mouthed the words "I'm sorry" but their meaning was obviously lost on her. Her gait was slow and deliberate. Her gown blew in the soft breeze and only then did he realize that he found her quite beautiful. But her grimace turned to scorn when she stopped in front of him. Unsure what to do next he gripped the scimitar tightly, ready to defend himself, but at the same time unwilling to harm a female. She glanced down at his weapon. His fingers gripped tighter still. She saw a bead of sweat drip from his brow signaling his fear. Raising the staff above her head again, Edgar saw the crystal flash with

energy. She said something in a loud clear voice and as she did his sword was invisibly pried from his hands, levitating in the air in front of him. He tried to snatch it from the air but it moved away from him faster than humanly possible. He watched as the scimitar glided through the sky. It struck the ground in front of the beast, planting itself in the soil to the hilt.

Edgar's breath grew short. She brought the staff down gently and placed it on his forehead. He could feel a surge of energy as his eyes flashed and purple lightning filled his periphery. The light was unbearable and forced him to shut his eyes. When he opened them again he was kneeling in front of the corpse of the beast, next to the sword. He wanted to reach for the weapon but his body was paralyzed. But his eyes could still move. He glared around and saw that both circles of women were now approaching. Their chanting never ceased. The lead woman once again positioned herself in front of him, standing between his body and that of the creature. Again she placed the crystal staff onto his forehead, then moved it away from his face and placed it reverently onto the forehead of the slain animal. Purple lightning poured like liquid from the creature's face. It moved in straight lines towards Edgar, entering his eyes and blinding him with visions of the creature's life. The animal was the center of the women's lives. *And I ate the damn thing. What have I done?*

From his kneeling position he started to see that the creature was rising from its deathbed. He wanted to cry out but no sound would come. The lightning still connected them. And then it went out abruptly. Edgar could no longer feel his heart pounding against his chest. All was still. He tried to draw a breath but could not. As he thought that it might be time to pray he opened his eyes for the last time. But it was not his eyes that he saw through. He was looking through the eyes of the beast. He looked upon himself and saw what was once his body slouch then crumple to the floor. The chanting of the women reached a fervor. He gazed up from his corpse and saw the reproduction of his craft. The woman with the staff approached the facsimile and raised the staff. Again purple lightning shot from the staff, igniting the twigs and branches. Through the creature's eyes he saw the mimicry go up in flames, lighting up the night sky. He looked through the "window" of the craft where the effigy of him had stood. Instead of a man made of sticks he saw his own form, fear stained face, gasping from the smoke. As his senses faded he could hear the faint cries of the man that had once been him, dying in the flames.

Collection Point

Dain Luscombe

Illustrations

Austin Hart

———●———

The platform began moving forward with very little noise and John started sweating in his air-conditioned spacesuit. The colorless slab was riding on a single rail fifteen centimeters wide at most. The featureless track wasn't connected to any support beams or struts and didn't look as if it could support any weight at all, yet astronaut John Shumer was moving slowly forward. He kneeled on the five foot square platform, his body poised to strike.

"I'm ten meters from the entrance."

The com crackled with a reply, "Copy that."

Shumer looked back at the micro-filament line extending from his heavy saddle bag. The wire reeled out slowly but was never slack, as a computer program let it out at a regulated rate. It was so thin he could only see it when the sun glinted off its surface. *My lifeline* he thought and sighed into his space helmet. This "lifeline" was one of the host of last ditch efforts to keep contact with the astronauts as they entered the alien craft. They had lost thirty two drone rovers and six humans to the alien cylinder within two months of it appearing on Earth. Each had entered through the same round orifice Shumer was heading towards. Not a scrap had returned. The orifice immediately closed after each astronaut entered and signals of every conceivable kind had failed to escape from within. The hope was that the micro-filament line would be thin enough that it would not be severed when the aperture closed, locking Shumer inside.

The gaping mouth of the craft loomed and the rail he was riding on disappeared in a curtain of darkness just inside the door. The midday sun made the contrast complete and Shumer rode his unstoppable train forward until he was enveloped in darkness.

"Switching on suit lights." he choked as he finished the sentence knowing the orifice was closing behind him and assuming he would get no reply.

The radio buzzed with a "We copy Shumer, good lu..." Silence.

A red light lit up in his helmet's display and he felt the saddle bag vibrate as it reeled in the severed lifeline.

'Zzzzzzzip' as the computer controlled reel finished its business. Shumer thought it was a stupid idea anyway.

His body was tense and controlled, he wasn't like the others and he knew it. The first humans inside had been scientists, boasting more degrees than you could list and trained in every conceivable aspect of a first contact mission. By comparison, Shumer's first contact training was maybe catching a few minutes of an old Star Trek episode before switching over, so he could enjoy the football game. He was woefully unprepared for things to go right but couldn't be more ready for things to fall apart. He was a decorated soldier before he joined NASA and had survived some intense scrapes without losing his cool.

The suit lights illuminated the featureless alcove with the platform rail spanning from one wall to another aperture identical to the one he had just passed through. As the platform continued forward, he noticed some debris below. It looked to be the remains of three or four of the AI rovers. On the second week, mission control had sent the robots in pairs, one on the moving platform and another to try to obstruct the orifice before it cut off radio contact. The desperate scientists had to watch their expensive robots fight a slow, losing battle with the aperture as it slowly and methodically cut them in two without showing the least resistance. Other than the debris the room was empty and the rate of motion was slow enough for Shumer to carefully dip into his bag. He brought out a heavy set of clamps with glowing electronics attached and leaned back to reach the rail behind his platform. With a clunk the clamps attached and a green light lit up in his helmet's display. This was a special transmitter that used powerful low frequencies that were then modulated with his voice. Scientists waited outside the craft with delicate sensors attached to the rail hoping to receive the vibrations with his message attached. They were supposed to send a

response signal showing there was a connection, but Shumer didn't expect to see that light turn green. It never did. He was on his own.

In the next chamber, a glowing light began to pulse, infusing the shadows with some unknown color, or perhaps all colors? A lifetime of combat expertise told Shumer that this was it.

Whatever was going to happen to him was happening now. He reached in his bag for his last and most desperate communication device. His fingers crept over the grip that was carefully holstered on the side of the bag. It looked like a firearm, almost shotgun sized, but it was a possible lifeline to the world outside the craft. It was a compact missile launcher for a tiny dart-sized projectile with enough powerful propellant that it could puncture almost any armor and survive. Then, instead of exploding as a normal missile, it would transmit a message to the crew waiting for it outside. He primed the audio recorder to begin its message the second he spoke and end the recording when he pulled the trigger. Shumer had been told to use this method only if all hope of return was lost. It was incredibly crude and could possibly be seen as a threat, but at this point they needed any information they could get.

His eyes gradually adjusted to the unnatural light throbbing on the other side of the room. It was a viscous cloud-like radiance, diffusing in every direction. He began to piece together an outline of something sharing the space with him. A glowing mass appeared to be clinging to the ceiling and much of the back wall. Moist tendrils extended in every direction, wafting in the still air of the room in a drowsy way. Whatever it was, the thing was clearly alive. For a moment, he thought the light from the creature was getting brighter, but soon realized one of the tendrils was reaching toward him. The platform he stood on moved ever forward and Shumer quickly looked for an escape route. As he searched the room he realized the ground level was again strewn with debris, but this time it wasn't all robotic. He was staring at the remains of the six humans sent into the craft and once he recovered his senses he noticed the end of the creature's tendril was centimeters from his helmet. He brought the missile launcher up between the creature and his helmet and was about to shout into the recorder's microphone when the creature's arm easily punctured the perspex face plate. Suddenly John Shumer's pulse rate dramatically slowed and his entire body relaxed.

Forty-eight seconds later, the projectile dart punctured the outer wall of the ship and effortlessly plunged its way through the twenty meters of carbon nano-tube layered concrete that the scientists had erected to catch it. The short audio clip was received and the General pulled on a pair of headphones. It was the first information to leave the alien craft since its arrival. It was the last word any one would ever hear from astronaut John Shumer. The recording began with a short gasp, and then a few moments of silence.

John Shumer's voice whispered "Beautiful".

Through the Raven's Eyes

———•———

Gabriel Hart

———•———

Illustrations

Austin Hart

A suffocating hush choked out the anxious, bustling chatter at the control consoles at NASA Kennedy Space Center. It spread like a silencing wave to the farthest operative corners of the large room, as its blinks, bleeps and bloops continued on, almost mocking the severity of the scene unfolding. This wave then ebbed backwards to its origin, Don Nicholes, who had his hand turned toward his co-workers to communicate a halt to all talk.

"There's no signal. This is bad," he continued, "These small seconds of silence may need to graduate to one proper, mourning minute…"

This tragedy would finally spill the beans to the public regarding NASA's clandestine branch and its airtight, guarded shadow missions, as they watched their longest-standing prospect fail, this time fatally. Years back, in 2014, after successfully passing Pluto and its moon system, the ever-enduring Voyager 1 had finally cleared the ice-laden Kuiper Belt into the farthest reaches of our solar system. Concurrently with its launch in 1977, in an experimental effort to test human mortality and endurance in our ever-accelerating times, NASA had created a top secret, potentially *kamikaze* style manned spacecraft named RATO RAVEN. RATO stood for "Rocket Assisted Take-Off," a term coined by Jack Parsons, who drew the blueprints for the craft before his explosive demise in 1952. The RATO RAVEN was the first vessel of subsequent NASA shadow missions; the idea being to see if human passengers could potentially outwit and repair any folly that may befall the Voyager 1 not far ahead of them. The RAVEN's collective human-soul and mere proximity would be the key driving force behind this controversial logic, beyond the tech-advancements the crew would come to inherit, learn, and utilize from the ever-evolving Earth behind them.

A crew of ten young, daring upstarts had been trained for this since their infancy in order to accommodate their lifespans, in relation to the undetermined length of the mission. Force-fed an education that would erase their childhoods, they would finally blast off in the demure primer-black RAVEN, into the black of space, undetectable to sight but not to radar. It was launched on September 5th, 1977, tandem in time with Voyager 1, though not location. RATO RAVEN flew from Groom Dry Lake in Nevada, known to most as Area 51, where these shadow missions continue to be launched today. Unfortunate to most conspiracy theorists, the disappearance of RATO RAVEN would also expose nothing beyond Area 51's simple commitment to unorthodox space exploration, debunking any arcane egg-headed notions of alien autopsies, their existence on Earth, or beyond.

While it was launched from Nevada, the mission's monitoring would eventually be inherited by a special team at Kennedy Space Center in Florida, where they witnessed the unceremonious end to the RAVEN'S 43-year path in stifling depression, confusion and defeat. Don Nicholes stood manikin-still, hunched over his console, his head hanging low like overripe fruit about to drop.

Of all the twenty-year-old men who first boarded the RAVEN for their ambitious mission of no return, only one had divided his training enough to let the distraction of love into his heart. But when Thomas Miller eloped with his wife, Judy, a month before the blast off, they both knew it was more symbolic than a legal binding. An anchor to keep them connected in mind rather than body, the two were young enough to still be seduced by the delusions of life-long romance. It was easier for Judy to justify such a potentially morbid commitment to an invisible husband after her Mother reassured her in context.

"It's not much different than when your father went to war and I thought I might never see him again," she said, "Only Thomas is about to embark on the single most ambitious call of duty the world has ever known. Imagine – you'll be the only wife on Earth that can carry that distinction."

Thomas' main area of expertise was radio communication, and it would be his focus to upgrade the RAVEN's signal through the years, with assistance of another team at JPL since the Voyager was unmanned and finite in its capabilities. To include Judy in his isolated professional life, he taught her everything he knew about astro-communication, often as he himself learned. This helped forge a bond between them that they hoped would stretch through the stars. He built her a state-of-the-art radio telescope, helping her devise a special code only the two of them would know and use, in the backyard of their stand-alone Nevada home, twenty miles outside Pahrump, Nevada.

Don Nicholes was Thomas' best friend since childhood. Don would keep in close contact with Judy, and assist her with upgrades to her dish through the years, so she could continue receiving messages from her husband. Always erratic, often fragmented and difficult to piece together, the radio communication with Thomas gave their long distance marriage a sense of adventure, intrigue and surprise when she would receive a message. While not for everyone, this curious union managed to fill enough of a void to keep Judy steadfast to never marry again.

Don slowly shook his dangling head and opened his eyes after two long minutes.

"I've got to call Judy."

Judy Miller jumped a bit when she heard her landline ring.

She didn't get calls often, as her support system consisted of two local ladies her age, and she hoped it wasn't Don calling this early. It could only be bad news. She prepared herself.

"Hello, this is Judy?"

"Judy? Don here…" he paused, "Uhm, Judy… Tom's gone. The ship has vanished the way of the Voyager. I think this is it. I can't process it, and I am sorry I have to be the one to tell you…

"Judy.

"Judy, are you there…?"

She gently put the phone back on the hook as she went slack-jawed. Catatonic. Remembering she had an apple in her hand, she took another forced, apathetic bite. She stared out the window at the desert nothingness to fiend for some epiphany of time and cycles and life and death and disintegration and reincarnation and how everything is exactly how it's supposed to be.

She got nothing in return.

Then, she felt guilty for the unspeakable sub-emotions she entertained: Was she finally free of a lifetime of empty loyalty? Or was Thomas dead to her the second he kissed her goodbye in September of 1977? As Judy grieved a myriad of ways, she felt both shame and confusion – that Thomas' heroic passing didn't feel much different than him not being there in the flesh anyway. It was impossible to reconcile. Exhausted from the confounded nature of mourning, she fell asleep, into the arms of darkness as the sun set through the window behind her.

She awoke to the sound of her console receiving a message from the dish pointed at the heavens. This time, she really jumped, running over to the desk.

It was Thomas! Did this mean he was alive?

Judy,

Never before have I prayed harder you would receive a mes-sage from me as this one, as I don't know where me and the crew's fate stands. I am writing, above all, to let you know that I love you and I always will, no matter what happens... We have lost control of our ship's path and are being pulled towards a beam of light larger than I could ever describe. I can only assume we will perish there, as we see clusters of debris bursting into flames as it reaches its, well, surface, I guess?

I can tell you I love you in a million different ways, but I need to spend some time letting you know exactly what I have pieced together out here. As I can only trust you will believe me. If I told Don or anyone at NASA, it would seem the ravings of a madman. So, since you had the courage to take this leap of faith when you married me forty years ago, I know you have the courage to suspend your belief in everything we have been taught about our universe.

After we passed the unspeakable vastness of the Kuiper Belt, we saw a tangible curve slightly demurred in the distance. Now, Judy... I hope you don't think I am obscene, but it resembled a perfect crystalline depiction of... well, I don't want to say depiction, because Judy... it was a detailed vision of a woman's genitalia. Now, I didn't exactly see this as much as I was given a psychic download of information from God knows where... As if my mind was trying to make sense of something that was larger than I could conceive, and this... well, gigantic vagina... is how it pieced it all together. Yet, it was reversed, as if we were about to leave..

Now, stay with me here, please... All of a sudden, like in dreams, where there at times seems to be an alternate, parallel understanding into something you are experiencing for the first time, this information continued to download into me, though it felt like it was inside me already, for my whole life. Do you remember that time we did LSD together? It was a lot like that, when we felt that oneness, that cellular connection with everything. But the specific answer has been bestowed onto me now. It came to me as a dron-

ing noise, and "OM" if you will... and it was through this buzz of all encompassing sound that I was given this rapturous information.

Sweetheart, I am writing you from the end of our universe, our universe which is the womb of a celestial feminine cavity inside an even larger, inconceivable body. I can confirm this with a unique fusing of my mind, heart and soul, which only you know the depths of.

I began to know that all these clusters of stars, all these distant galaxies are none other than divine ejaculations of future life. It was a mere gut feeling I had, until we saw this beam of light approaching... and we now see it emitting endless streams of what I understand to be vaporous carbon, and we can see it all forming into more substantial solids the longer we pay attention, which is difficult, being that we have lost control and are being pulled to this light. This might very well be our demise. Of us as we know it, anyway...

But sweetheart, my point is... like all the planets in our system, our Earth is an egg, and it was lucky enough to be formed by the ultimate culmination of this process, and able to sustain us as the only life in the solar system. We are merely the Earth's essential bacteria. Only as we know, bacteria can also turn bad.

Humans are on Earth to fertilize the Earth as an egg, so it can finally give birth to everything it has to offer from inside. Is it any surprise to you that all of that molten center has the ability to act as a yolk or a fetus, to continue the quest for spreading life? But we don't know for sure. We haven't been to the center of the Earth, because we are too busy exploring space. Like idiots, Judy. It is my regret to say, that all this time, we have been going the wrong direction... By exploring space, we are willfully abandoning our true path into the Earth. And the worst part - that we couldn't abort this mission even if we tried. By its very nature, our mission itself is the abortion!

And look at how the Earth is being treated. Its crust is drying at such accelerated rates that the surface fertilization may never occur. We have found ourselves trying to take care of something stillborn from neglect. The birth of its inside, its soul.

Our planet is one of the solar system's last chances. All the other planets seem nearly poisoned by the same process, once inhabited by those just like us who didn't know the glory of where they stood, and neglected it as such. Whether it created atmospheres of suffocating gas, thousand year storms, or an arid wasteland where no water could form, it was all a result of bacteria just like us, turning toxic, destroying one another like the cancer we on Earth would later not only create, suffer from, but also emulate. Sure, we multiplied, but at too fast of a rate to realize our one job on Earth! We mutated, rather than grew. Homogenous, mirror images of each other, making the same mistakes. And on those other planets, the slow evolution of cellular division with the tending of the ground, was never to be realized

And as I see large misshapen boulders of debris burning up into this colossal, glorious phallic-esque beam of light, demonstrating the crew and I's now merciful demise, of a mission that was doomed to failure by its very insistence, I think of one man responsible for all of this. Jack Parsons, the true Antichrist, the man who created rocket science via black magic, who drew the plans for this craft. A man who would eventually steer us so far off our natural God-given obvious path that only HE would convince the citizens of the world that flinging ourselves into the black empty void of outer space would be progress?!? The Devil! The great pretender! But who is more evil – he who pretends, or they who believe him!?!

I was supposed to stay with you, Judy. I was supposed to give you a child like God intended, to be fruitful and multiply, to continue our intentions of nurturing our planet. But here I am, in the fourth decade of abandoning my loving wife, while forcing her into some charade of hero worship. Here I am floating in space de-volved to a dead sperm, finally being put out of my misery!

But Judy, now I can only wish if a miracle finds me, and some-how takes me back to Earth and away from this lifetime of counter-intuitive nightmare, I vow to make love to you like I never have be-fore. But until that day of never, it is my solemn duty to leave you with this burden of truth."

Judy took one more bite of her apple and hung her head, drained from the surreal last dispatch from her phantom husband. She gazed out the window at the vastness of the desert, and slowly walked out the door to the backyard.

She grabbed the rusted shovel that had leaned against the shed for years, walked to the middle of the yard and jammed it into the ground with all her might. She exclaimed with a primitive grunt, punctuating every stab into the ground, until it was a foot deep. Now down to the apple's core, still in her hand, she dropped it into the hole, and began to return its soil. Since she knew it wouldn't rain for the rest of the year, Judy finally burst into tears over the hole, like a storm with nowhere to go.

The New Luddites

———•———

Mari Collier

———•———

Illustrations

Rik Verlin Livingston

———●———

Noah Beckam looked at the robo in front of him. It was a carbon copy of all the other unisex robos except its face was expressionless and it wore no clothes. Of course, there were no private areas to cover so clothes weren't necessary. It certainly wasn't going to feel cold or heat, at least not yet. It was a design still based on the first human like Amazon robot built in the twenty-first century.

This was the last station before being added to the column against the wall. The completed ones would be dispatched at fifteen minutes before closing bell.

Noah attached the UnitCord into the port behind the Robo's right ear and began the program. It took all of five minutes to download the artificial and voice intelligence (AIVI). Now the testing could begin.

"Your name is Bendle 15," Noah said. "That is what you will respond to when someone gives you a direction or order. Can you answer to Bendle 15?"

"Of course, I can. Why are you asking such an inane question? In fact, what is your name? Can you respond to a simple question or follow an order?"

Noah looked at the hunk of soft plastic, ceramics, and wires in front of him. He had heard the AIVI program had been updated, but this verged on outrageous. It seemed as though that thing thought for itself. What was AIVI Corp's headquarters planning?

NOAH
ZONO ART
Bendle 15

Bendle 15 continued, "I am your superior multiplied many times over. This is the floor I am designed to run. You are but a paid worker with no ability to grow in your mind or your abilities. How long do you think you'll last?" It laughed at him and sauntered, actually sauntered, toward the row of robos waiting along the wall for their assignment.

Noah gritted his teeth as the next robo approached his workspace ready for the AIVI software. His heart was hammering. If what Bendle 15 said was true, everyone in this department would be out of a job like those on the lower floors and the thousands of truck drivers, train engineers, bus drivers, and taxi drivers displaced by electric self-running vehicles. Robo police officers and a few human police officers were chasing the displaced workers from the streets and protest areas.

Noah grabbed the marble paperweight he had been given for his participation in the AIVI program and hurled it at Bendle 15. It struck him in the knees and took him to the floor. Noah picked up his ergonomic chair and bashed it down on Bendle 15's back and head, over and over again until the soft plastic imploded and sizzled from the electrical circuits inside. The Bendles 1 through 14 regarded him, but made no aggressive movement. They weren't programed for fighting. The floor alarm bells began ringing and the robo voice came over the system: Alert! Alert! Emergency, Floor 5 Room 3. It repeated, and repeated.

Noah ran for the door and for the stair fire escape. The building was so ancient the equipment for human safety was still installed. He smashed the glass covering the Exit button and pushed, praying the door would open as the robo guards swarmed through the elevator door running towards the room he had just left. They had been given orders to go to that room. Unlike a human counterpoint, the robo guard could not deviate from a direct order and Noah headed out the door. He swung the stairs downward and took them as fast as possible. He was in the alley and started to walk towards the front when he heard sirens.

If there were still humans in one of the police cars, they would spot him. He ran back to a cross alley and ran for two blocks before venturing out towards the street. He knew the company would give the authorities his address. He was a wanted man. He had just destroyed a $350,000.00 company product. The truck drivers' union was a few blocks away. Could he make it without being caught? It had been built when real people still drove trucks. If he stayed out after nightfall, there was always the danger that someone would report him as a man still in workday clothing.

He tried to keep his face bland as he walked purposely toward his objective. He didn't want a security camera showing a fleeing felon, a destroyer of company products. He marched up to the woman in an orange bodysuit handing out flyers to anyone that passed; a futile task. Most of the "people" out walking were robos going to some directed place. Where were the others usually crowded around here?

He took the flyer and was about to walk away when he saw a robo cop marching across the street at the crosswalk half-a-block away. He ducked his head, pretending to read what was on the flyer.

The woman was clever and yelled out to the empty street, "That's all for today, folks." She reached back and pushed the door open and Noah rushed inside. She followed him and hit the secure lock.

"Thank you," Noah gasped.

"You're welcome, but they do scan the security cameras every fifteen minutes. You'll have to go out the back way."

"They'll see that too." Noah's voice was bitter.

"Just why are the robos after you?"

"It isn't the robos, it is the entire force. I destroyed one of the newest AIVI robos at Bendle."

Her mouth fell open. "That was you?"

"I would have destroyed the AIVI unit if it had been on that floor." Noah looked at her.

"Where are your companions? I thought another march was due today," he asked.

"They were all rounded up last night and imprisoned. Don't you read the News on MS or Google?"

"I've been busy," Noah muttered.

"Ha, you're a game player or a streamer and pay current events no mind. Now you have to leave or they'll be after me too."

"And where do you suggest I go? Don't you people have a safe place?" He saw the hesitation in her eyes, and then she shrugged.

"There is no safe place anymore. Humans are doomed, but come with me and we'll keep them puzzled this afternoon." She led the way towards the back and opened a door with a stair leading down.

"They may not know this is here. If you go down below, use your pad or tablet to light the way. Keep walking in a straight line." She hesitated. "Can you return to your apartment?"

"Of course not. They know where I live." He drew in a breath. "I know you were a trucker and weren't keeping tabs on what was happening here."

"Wrong. I was in the dispatch office until it wasn't needed anymore. The routes are all planned through AIVI coordinates, except there is less and less demand since humans can't afford to buy unnecessary things. Robos don't need food, they don't need clothes, and they don't need toys. They are using different methods to destroy all humans, in a humane way, of course."

Noah swallowed. "The AIVI needs to be destroyed! Isn't there any place where someone is planning to destroy AIVI headquarters?"

"Man, are you crazed? How do you plan on getting inside? How would you survive until you reached the center of the operations?"

"First I have to find a safe place. Just get me out of here. I'll make it."

She looked at him. "All right, follow me. By the way, I'm Carla Anderson," she said as she grabbed her backpack from the desk and started down the stairs.

"I'm Noah Beckham," Noah responded and followed her downward.

Carla snapped on her belt's tab light and led the way. Noah noted there seemed to be several paths leading in different directions. How long had this underground domain existed? Then he realized it was like a lot of old cities. This was a built-over area and the paths were once streets or roads. How did Carla even know of their existence?

She led him to a ladder hung with chains. "We climb here," she said and started upward. Noah followed. She pushed a panel and crawled through with Noah right behind her. They were in a dimly lit room filled with boxes.

"This is where our union books are stored. It's also a homeless shelter," she explained. "Let's go up and I'll introduce you to the others."

Noah followed behind her. Homeless, that is what he was now, or in jail if found. The former sounded better. The jail guards were all robos. Some claimed the judges were robos too, but if so, they were superior to those he had been creating. He touched her arm, "Will I have to register?"

"No, not for just visiting." She opened the door.

They stepped into a kitchen and the people working there ignored them as they walked through. Carla led him to a table in the back and a large, dark man with tight curled hair and brown eyes rose and hugged Carla. "We saw the cast where the robo cops raided our last outpost. Did you set the detonator below?"

"Of course, I did," Carla replied and hugged him back. "It may or may not be on the news tonight. AIVI doesn't like it when we wipe out some of the robos." She turned to Noah.

"Brinkley, meet Noah. Let's just leave it on a first name basis for now, but if you saw the earlier cast you know who he is and why he is here."

Brinkley narrowed his eyes and nodded. "Why not get a cup of coffee," he suggested, "and then come back. We need to have a discussion."

Noah obediently followed Carla. "You have coffee?" He was in awe.

"Imitation, but sometimes it's real." They grabbed a cup and went back to the table.

Brinkley looked at Carla. "How do you know this is the real deal? He might be a robo plant and get us all thrown in jail."

Carla took a sip before answering. "He was definitely on the run from the robos and they were after someone. I saw that cast. I don't believe they would have let him destroy such a valuable robo just to fake us out."

"How do we know the robo was the expensive one?"

"Brinkley, did you see the cast at 3:15 or a later one?

"It was a later one," he admitted. "They just announced that one Noah Beckham was wanted for destroying the newest Bendle Robo model."

"One with installed AIVI," Noah gritted out. "I was the installer and that piece of machinery informed me that I would no longer be necessary. I-I-I lost it." Noah hid his face in his hands, took a deep breath, and looked up. "But I'd do it again. I should have destroyed each and every one of them, but the Robo Security was coming and I ran for it."

"How did you get out if Security was alerted?"

"AIVI never had an emergency like that. The old emergency exits for fires were still available for the human personal. I used one of them. They will probably close those off now if humans are no longer in the building."

"I'm surprised they were using such an old building for something so important," said Brinkley.

Noah shrugged. "It's like they don't need new buildings. AIVI just masses the robos together when not in use. Why build new buildings when you can utilize the old. Getting wet or cold doesn't bother a robo."

A man in beige, baggy coveralls and same colored shirt appeared. He had a scarf tied over his head, effectively hiding the hair color. He nodded at Brinkley and motioned with his head to indicate the conversation should be private.

"It's okay, Lem. Noah has just joined us," said Brinkley as he looked up. "Noah, this is Lem. We just use one name here."

Noah started to rise. "I can leave if you like."

"No, stay. You'll learn what you will be doing." Brinkley scooted out a chair for Lem. "How did it go?"

"Not good. The robos placed in human positions, don't need a bathroom. They don't need breaks, and they don't get sent home. We don't know which transport to attack as we don't have that kind of scanner. It's getting eerie out there. We just missed that mass of security robos around Carla's office. They had been whisked off in an electric robocar. All we saw were humans crushing into a store that doesn't have enough supplies."

"It looks like we are being pushed into mass extinction," came Carla's bitter words. "I say we burn everything."

"That leaves us with nothing," Brinkley reminded her.

Noah cleared his throat. "Do you know of any way to get rid of the AIVI that is directing everything? What happened to our decision makers in DC? Did they all abdicate?"

"They, like all the countries, have let AIVI run the world. AIVI has no reason to fight over land or money. Those things are meaningless, so all nuclear weaponry and missiles have been destroyed. All armies are staffed with robos which are not paid. That means more men and women wandering around in our cities looking for jobs or robos to destroy. When caught doing any destruction, they are jailed in apartment buildings and guarded by robos."

Brinkley looked at Noah. "Haven't you been getting any news?"

Noah's face flushed. "Ah, I guess I was too busy playing games when I wasn't working." He leaned forward. "Whenever I ordered food or any item, it was always promptly delivered. I thought everything was running smoothly."

"It is for people with jobs and money. The former which you no longer have and your bank account has probably been frozen. All done electronically, of course." The last sentence was almost snorted out.

Lem stood. "I'll let you educate this child. I need some food. I say we start another riot."

"We can't," Clara broke in. "You know that. They'll take away the food from here and we can't get into their warehouses."

"That is the problem. All of us are afraid of dying all at once instead of this slow day by day death we are enduring." Lem stomped off.

Noah turned back to the other two. "Is it really that bad? What about the areas where they still grow food?"

"Robos don't need food," Brinkley snorted. "It's difficult for an agriculturalist to make enough money to buy seed to replant. Some have been using the seeds from the ripe plants to grow their own food. The cattle, hogs, chickens, turkeys, and sheep pretty much run loose. The environmentalists were delighted until they realized the cattle, sheep, and hogs were destroying the land. They don't know what to do about it as it would mean penning them up or destroying them. Humans dying doesn't bother them."

Noah was sitting open mouth. He shook his head. "Why does AIVI permit humans to die?"

"AIVI sees no need for humans. The Environmentalists took over the Progressive Party and were able to put in their directive to control the amount of human births. The population has been diminishing since then. With AIVI in control that will continue. The

Environmentalists thought they had succeeded in ending all oil exploration and drilling, but since oil is needed to produce plastics for new robos and repair that has continued."

"How do we stop AIVI?"

This time they looked at Noah like he was mad. Noah looked at them and continued. "I am serious. Where is AIVI housed? The main unit, I mean. I realize it is connected electronically across our country, but there has to be one main source. I'm guessing it is still right here in DC government buildings."

"You can't be serious. It is protected by all sorts of security."

Noah nodded. "Yeah, like electronics and robos controlled by AIVI. What happens when the lights go out?"

"They wouldn't," Brinkley responded. "It's solar, plus fuel cells in the wall, and it has battery backup. You're dreaming."

"Anyone ever thought of going underground?" Noah asked.

"What good would a mole do?" Brinkley snapped. "They don't need humans in that place."

"I'm not talking about working there. I'm talking about attacking from underground upward. You'd have to have special equipment and protective gear, but it would work better than a frontal attack, or one from above. If you give me some time, I think I can present something that works. First I need a diagram of the place and the streets around it. Once we are in, we can disable the wiring that goes through the walls. It won't matter how much electricity flows if the wires aren't there to carry it up or outward."

"You'd be in a suicide situation. They would send a robo security force."

"Then we best pray we cut their communications lines."

Brinkley sat back. "Do you really think we can do that?"

"What other options do you or anyone else have? It's either die gloriously or ingloriously." Noah doubled his fist.

"If there is a riot or protest going on outside that would divert their attention." Carla felt she was adding the obvious. "No one can produce a protest better than our Unions."

"They might not agree if they know what we are doing." Brinkley's face looked thoughtful. "I think they give the Unions food to distribute just to keep the former workers quiet."

Noah took a deep breath. "Are you able to pull all the information I asked for without alerting them?"

Brinkley pondered a minute. "You know, if we go to the records at the Construction Hall, they would have that on their own Central file. We wouldn't need to do a search where we broach AIVI's security. It might be a bit outdated as far as the outside goes, but the underground should be pretty much the same. I'm not sure what the wiring of the place would show without seeing it."

"How far is this Hall?"

"You're in luck, Noah. It's in the next building."

Noah followed Brinkley and Carla into the next building and down into the storage area. An attendant was inside a small office.

"Hello, Dickson, this is our new Luddite. The Security Robos are after him, but he may have a plan to solve our problems."

Dickson looked at Noah, surprise on his face. "Really, and you come to a storage area to implement it?"

"Nice to meet you, too," Noah muttered.

Dickson shrugged. "Likewise. It's a good hiding spot down here at least."

Brinkley grinned. "We're not here to hide. We need to look at plans for the Governmental Center of Information created fifty years ago. They still used blueprints on the location at that time. Can you locate them for us? Like right now?"

Dickson shook his head. "You're all mad. Carla, are you really a part of this? I thought your position was secure."

"Like the rest of you, I'm now being hunted. Or would be if I returned to what I was doing." She pointed her index finger at him. "We all need to be part of this."

"Mad, you are all mad. Wait here. I'll be right back." He walked down one of the many aisles of files and found 2125 Government Buildings and pulled out a drawer bin. "Someone want to give me a hand?" He yelled to the front. "There's more here than I thought."

Brinkley, Noah, Carla, and Dickson all carted the files to the long table and began to open everything. "Does anyone have plain paper?" Noah asked.

"What's that? It's always printed on if there is any distributed. We have to use our tablets, remember." Carla frowned at him.

"AIVI controls all the tablets. We can't put anything on ours." Noah replied.

"Wait," Dickson commanded. He ran to the back and returned lugging a box. "This is filled with reams of unneeded paper. It missed the burning pile. It seems the AIVI doesn't want mere humans using paper. They can't scan it unless we post something or we are where their Security Cams are."

"Excellent, put those in a safe place," Brinkley advised. "When we're ready we'll copy and distribute if necessary, but even then we will need to be careful."

"We'll need to take a look at the surrounding area also, but somehow keep AIVI from knowing we are doing it or why we would be interested."

"That will be tricky. Physical maps haven't been around for years. Anything in the old books is outdated. An observer on the ground is your only option. You might want to start that now." Dickson was full of advice.

"I can do that," said Carla. "I'll check and see about tourist tours. They always have those for anyone that still thinks this is a great way to live. I'll be back in a day or two." She returned to the other building.

Brinkley, Noah, and Dickson began reading the old blueprints. Everything was spelled out in what contractors called specs. It listed how thick the foundation, the walls, and the flooring would be. It listed the materials to be used, and all the dimensions. The wiring specifications were on another set.

The subterranean portion was huge. It was as though the original builders knew how much the building would be expanded and enlarged in the coming decades and the huge blocks with the cement reinforced rebar walls seemed to laugh at their idea of breaking through from below. Noah was baffled. How could mere men do something that was mostly constructed by men and early robotic tools?

"What's that?" Noah pointed to a diagram of a drain running down from the bottom into the earth. The flooring around it had figures indicating it would be a little lower than the rest of the floor.

"It looks like they would be draining water out of there into the ground, but why would they worry about water down there? It can't seep through walls that thick." Dickson was puzzled and Brinkley was frowning.

"You'd think a dehumidifier would remove any excess moisture." Brinkley mused.

"Were the dehumidifiers that efficient when it was built?" Noah asked.

"We don't know," Brinkley admitted. "Yet it looks like the weakest spot in the floor. We could go up there and then drill around it to open it up." Brinkley was staring down at the plans. "Drilling is the only way we could break through once we are beneath there. We can only hope they have not installed new sensor programs that far below."

Dickson looked at him. "And just where would you get drilling robos without being detected?"

"We don't use robos. We use humans. They can't have destroyed all those old tools."

Dickson sat back. "The only place you would find old tools is in a museum somewhere and they wouldn't run without some sort of electrical supply. The older ones have no need for electricity. Men drilled or pounded them into the rock and then used explosives, which aren't available to humans either."

Brinkley glared at him and then his face cleared. "Dickson, I could hug you! You just solved our problem. Somehow we'll hijack the juice to those old tools."

Dickson looked dubious. "There's no guarantee they will work."

"It doesn't matter. It could take us over a year to break through, but once we do. We can disable everything. Does anyone know where to look for an older, electrical engineer that could help us with that?"

Dickson smiled at them. "Of course, my grandfather. He worked on the project."

"If you think of anyone that can get their hands on the demolition products, let us know."

"Brinkley, the demolition products are for the robo miners, period. There is nothing out on the market to buy unless you a certified company with a robo crew."

Brinkley nodded. "Then we go with what we have. I'm betting some of those old subway tunnels that aren't used anymore are our route of access. Everyone will have to help and be prepared for a long, winter."

"At least the temperature should be moderate underground." Dickson smiled at them. "Me, I have to stay here. They might send in a robo if I'm absent. We don't want them messing around in our paperwork."

It took months of research and digging to find where the drainage from the Complex went into the ground. They were like moles, so accustomed to the darkness of earth that they had to shield their eyes from any light, but the jubilation of breaking through was held inside while they waited to hear bells or warning robo voices, but silence greeted and held them.

Their meeting was held underground and Brinkley gave his orders. "Carla, you need to have Dickson bring his grandfather here. We don't want to touch the wrong thing.

Carla had her runners relay the message to Dickson. Within two days, she was introducing Sam Dickson to Brinkley. The man walked with a limp, his white hair was almost nonexistent, and it was a given that all of his teeth were implants. His brown eyes took in the scene of the underground chamber and widened.

"I didn't think I would ever see this again. Over there is where we used to eat before going above and installing more wires." He turned to Brinkley. "I can't lie to you. This might not work. Humans didn't install the last three levels. They had robos doing that."

"Who gave the robos the layout for those levels?" Brinkley asked.

"The AIVI did. It was powerful even then. I was called in to check a couple of things and found two errors. The robos responsible were destroyed. The ones that made the errors in placement and the ones who did the installing. New ones were sent in to check everything. I presumed that was to have the layout embedded in their memory banks."

"Why were the others destroyed? They could have been reprogrammed." Carla was puzzled.

"Maybe the AIVI felt they were flawed. I don't know. I was paid and dismissed," the old man answered. He set about checking the wiring and carefully disabling the room, before moving on to the next. The crew dragged their boxes and lights with them. It was in the middle room that Sam Dickson called the leaders and group to hear what would happen next.

"This is actually the first room where the wires were installed. The wires here lead to every room in this facility, even the upper most ones were connected to those below. You must keep a way clear and lighted for us to escape when I bring it all down. Even if

"We're FREE!"

the escape route is there, we may all die. You will also need a leader or someone on the outside to explain to the world what has happened. I don't matter. I've lived my life and this is my revenge." He limped to one side of the room and signaled for a younger man to help lift and remove a wall panel.

On the inside was a white plaque with red lettering: Danger Beware.

A grim smile etched itself onto Sam's face and he studied the switches and wires. Occasionally he nodded. Then he began to disengage the wires and push at the switches. After ten minutes the sirens began. Bells were clanging somewhere and pounding was heard on the locked doors.

"I've disabled the electronic locks," he muttered. "Knock out those staircases."

The room plunged into darkness and then relit with the gear that Brinkley had assigned. "Out, now!" Sam yelled.

The younger members started to run. Noah remembered Sam and helped to guide him out, down, and then upward again. They could hear explosions behind them and dust was filling the passage behind them when they emerged into the basement under an abandoned subway terminal.

"We need to get out of here," Noah yelled at those standing in the room.

It became a mad dash for the stairs leading upward as they jostled one another. An explosive detonating CL32 robo rolled through the opening from where Noah and Sam had just emerged and ignited. Darkness settled over the area and the ground level of the station shook.

Carla and Brinkley were shielding their eyes from the sunlight after reaching the ground floor when the explosions from the subterranean area shook the frame of the building. The building had been built in the early days of preventing earthquake or bombing attacks. It swayed, but didn't collapse.

Both raced to the door leading to the outside. Grime covered men and two women burst into the room from the basement stairwell. "It's done!" Matt Tipwan was yelling at them, "But something went wrong! There's more behind us." He and the other two kept running for the exit door.

Carla started for the stairwell door and Brinkley grabbed her arm. Another explosion shook the building and the frame around the stairwell cracked and splintered. "Out!" he yelled and pulled her towards the door to the street.

"What happened?" Carla demanded of Matt who like everyone else was staring at the building they had just left as it trembled and smoked.

Matt's eyes kept searching for a fire engine or robo cops, but none appeared. "Noah said Sam had cut the lines to the AIVI's lair and for everyone to leave. Sam couldn't move as fast and Noah was helping him. I was closest to the tunnel. We ran. They must have sent explosive drones before the last of the electricity was cut."

"Or the explosive were embedded in the structure," said Brinkley.

"Let's go before emergency vehicles arrive." He and Carla walked away.

"All my things were in there," said Carla.

"It can't be helped," Brinkley replied. "Look, there isn't any electricity to the traffic lights. They're dead." He pointed to a robo cop standing at the corner. It was inert. Its face blank. A man was trying to talk to it and finally shoved it over.

"We're free!" the man in coveralls shouted. "We're free!"

AUTHOR BIOS

———●———

Composer **Julie Carpenter** packed up the dog and husband and moved to the desert after their car broke down in Palm Springs one balmy July day, when they decided it was just the change they needed from chilly Los Angeles. Here, she continues making music with her project Less Bells and spying on the wildlife. She also writes sad stories set in the future.

———●———

Jon Christopher was born and raised in Southern California. He lives with his love of 35 years, Tania, and their dog Suki, in the hi-desert overlooking Joshua Tree National Park. Jon is the author of four novels, including his latest, *Joe's Late Great American Dream*, which was published in 2020 on Traveling Shoes Press. He describes himself a "creatively restless" and is either writing, creating music, painting or designing books... his latest project involves making videos and writing reviews of cannabis for Red Bench Reviews. jonandtania.com

———●———

Mari Collier was born on a farm in Iowa on a mattress her parents had made. It was covered with an oil cloth. The farm where she grew up had no electricity or inside bathroom. She has lived in Arizona, Washington, and Southern California. She and her husband, Lanny, met in high school and were married for forty-five years. She has served on the Board of

Directors for the Twentynine Palms Historical Society, and still serves as a Docent and writes a column for the Old Schoolhouse Museum. She has worked as a loan collector, bookkeeper, receptionist, and Advanced Super Agent for Nintendo of America. Her short stories have appeared in print and electronically, plus there are four anthologies. *Twisted Tales From The Desert, Twisted Tales From The Northwest, Twisted Tales From The Universe*, and *Twisted Tales From A Skewed Mind. Earthbound* is the first of the seven *Chronicles of the Maca* series. *Man, True Man* is the first of the three *Tonath Chronicles*. She is working on another anthology and a novel temporarily called *Thalia at War*. All of the anthologies have been translated into Spanish, Portuguese, and Italian. The first five of the Maca Chronicles have been translated into Italian and Spanish. The first three into Portuguese. *Earthbound, Gather the Children, Before We Leave, Return of the Maca*, and *Twisted Tales from The Northwest* are also Audible books. maricollier.com

———●———

Jean-Paul L. Garnier lives and writes in Joshua Tree, CA where he is the owner of Space Cowboy Books, a science fiction bookstore, independent publisher, and producer of *Simultaneous Times* podcast. In 2020 his first novella *Garbage In, Gospel Out* was released by Space Cowboy Books and in 2018 Traveling Shoes Press released *Echo of Creation*, a collection of his science fiction short stories. He has also released several collections of poetry: *In Iudicio* (Cholla Needles Press 2017), *Future Anthropology* (currently being translated into Portuguese), and *Odes to Scientists* (audiobook - Space Cowboy Books 2019). He is a two time Elgin Nominee and also appeared in the *2020 Dwarf Stars* anthology. His current collection of SF poetry, *Betelgeuse Dimming* was released in late 2020. He is also a regular contributor for Canada's *Warp Speed Odyssey* blog. His short stories, poetry, and essays have appeared in many anthologies and webzines. jplgarnier.blogspot.com

Brent A Harris is a two-time Sidewise Award finalist for alternate history who writes about dinosaurs, fantasy, the fears of our future and the mistakes of our past. He considers Southern California home, where he's become convinced that Joshua trees are in fact, real trees. When not writing speculative fiction, he focuses on his family, playing board games with friends, and talking nerdy to people. He holds a Masters degree in Creative Writing from National University as an NU Scholar. BrentAHarris.com

Gabriel Hart lives in Morongo Valley in California's High Desert. He's the author of the dipso-surrealist noir twin-novel *Virgins In Reverse / The Intrusion* (Traveling Shoes Press). His latest book, the Palm Springs crime-fiction novelette *A Return To Spring* (Mannison Press) was released in 2020. Other works have appeared in Pulp Modern, Shotgun Honey, ExPat Press, Bristol Noir, Black Hare Press (Australia), and Crime Poetry Weekly. He is a regular contributor to Lit Reactor, Econo-Clash Review, Space Cowboy's Simultaneous Times podcast, as well as L.A. Record, a Los Angeles underground music publication. Hart also taught the writing workshop for Mil-Tree, a non-profit reach out program for Vets and Active Duty Military to heal the wounds of war. mrgabrielhart.blogspot.com

Dain Luscombe is an American writer and composer whose work centers on humanity's reaction to emerging technologies. Some say that this was a result of being raised with silly notions of a future filled with flying cars and laser guns, but in truth he accidentally swallowed a Texas Instruments graphing calculator as a child, causing him to empathize with intelligent machines more than his fellow humans. He now resides in the Mojave Desert and awaits the end of the world.

Susan Rukeyser writes and reads in Joshua Tree. Previously, she bought bestsellers for Baker & Taylor, edited small-press book reviews for Necessary Fiction, and ran her own used bookshop. Her Creative Writing MA is from Lancaster University, UK. Her debut novel, *Not On Fire, Only Dying*, (Twisted Road Publications), was an SPD Fiction Bestseller. Space Cowboy Books published her prose chapbook, *Swap / Meet*. Some of her feminist science fiction was performed on the Simultaneous Times podcast: "From The Angels to Snakes" (Ep. 14), "We Have Your Connie Moody," (Ep. 18), and "The Ebb Somatic" (Ep. 29). Susan published *Feckless Cunt: A Feminist Anthology* and co-created The Desert Split Open Presents, Joshua Tree's queer, feminist, and otherwise radical open mic/author series. susanrukeyser.com

———●———

Anastasia Wasko is an artist, writer, and energy worker from (but not limited to) the New York/New Jersey area. With a BA in Transpersonal Psychology from Sofia University (formerly Institute of Transpersonal Psychology), her creative output is largely informed by psychosynthesis, depth psychology, clinical parapsychology, evolutionary psychology, and Tarot studies. Her fiction and creative non-fiction writing have appeared in Space Cowboy's *Simultaneous Times* podcast, *Thrive Global*, and in *Journal of Exceptional Experiences*. Her energy work practice EVOL focuses on reiki, homa, guided meditation, and astrological insight. Wasko spent several years working on Mindfield, the official publication of the Parapsychological Association. Her copyediting work has covered a wide range of material as well, from nanotechnology to anti-racist organizing. anastasiawasko.com

ARTIST BIOS

---•---

Austin Hart is an artist/designer from Laguna Beach, CA currently living in Morongo Valley. Inspired by Robert Crumb, and Carravagio he uses art to find interest in everyday people and places. He works across many mediums including oil, graphite and digital focusing at first on solid shapes and volumes until an idea reveals itself. "I love showing scale and depth and painting air. Exploring fantasy and sci-fi art has allowed me to push those concepts farther" austinarthurhart.com

---•---

Zara Kand is an American Symbolist painter based in Southern California. She has exhibited throughout numerous venues within the US and has been featured in many online and print publications. She currently lives in the California high desert where she spends most of her time oil painting, curating art shows, teaching painting classes, illustrating, and catering events. She is also the editor of *The Gallerist Speaks*, an interview series focusing on gallery owners, directors and curators. zarakand.com

---•---

Rik Verlin Livingston – I originally hail from Kansas and my first jobs were ranching and farming. I soon decided that painting and drawing were a whole lot less exhausting than ranching and farming. So I've made my living, for most of my life, in the field of art, rather than the fields of Kansas. As a kid, I answered an ad in the back of a comic book where you "Draw the Pirate," and took a correspondence course where you learn all about art (not!) Later, I got an Associate, Bachelor and Masters of Fine Art degrees, the last from the San Francisco Art Institute, a very old and respected establishment. None of those fine colleges asked me to draw a pirate, but I recently did, just for fun. I've taught at two San Francisco colleges. I've had three years of being Art Director for a 5,000 square foot cultural center in the Haight Ashbury, and a year or two as Art Director for the biggest Boys and Girl's Club west of the mighty Mississippi. But mostly, I've just made art. And, wow, I'm still not tired of it! I moved to Southern California in 2006-2008, and enjoy spending time in both the High Desert and Coachella Valley. A "Desert Valley Star" interview of me was titled "Out of His Mind." I'm not sure if they meant that in a Zen "no-mind" sense or not, but I'll take it as a compliment. I like art that is unusual and fun. You can see more of my art at ZonoArt.com (NOT your typical art site!)

Jeremy Szuder is a chef by night and creator of poetry and illustration work by day. His past track record in the arts includes; 15 years as a musician in various bands (drums, vocals), graphic design work for clothing/skateboard companies, 25 plus years of self-published Zines, showings of fine art in the underground art scene, a 10 year plus stint spinning vinyl at various events all across the city, and at present time continues to have both illustrations and poems published by over a dozen fine art and literary publications all across the U.S.A. as well as Canada. Jeremy Szuder continues to call Los Angeles California via Glendale his home at present. jeremyszuder.wordpress.com

Reagan Louise Wilson is a writer & artist who lives in Los Angeles with her two dogs & an abundance of sunflowers. In the Anthropocene her allegiance lies with the coyotes.

WARP SPEED
ODYSSEY

THE TWILIGHT ZONE
the AMAZING SPIDER
THE FANTASTIC
THINK I'M TR
BUT THEY
SUSPECT
REAL POW
ADDED ATTRACTION: SPIDE
CHAMELEC
BOR
HOME
by
McKENNA
THE SAND PEBBLES
LEIBER
RRY HARRISON
DO YOU WANT TO
TRAVEL BACK
IN TIME?
WWW.GALACTICJOURNEY.ORG

https://joe.travelingshoespress.com

MARI COLLIER

THALIA
THE NEW GENERATION

CHRONICLES OF THE MACA BOOK 7

https://www.maricollier.com

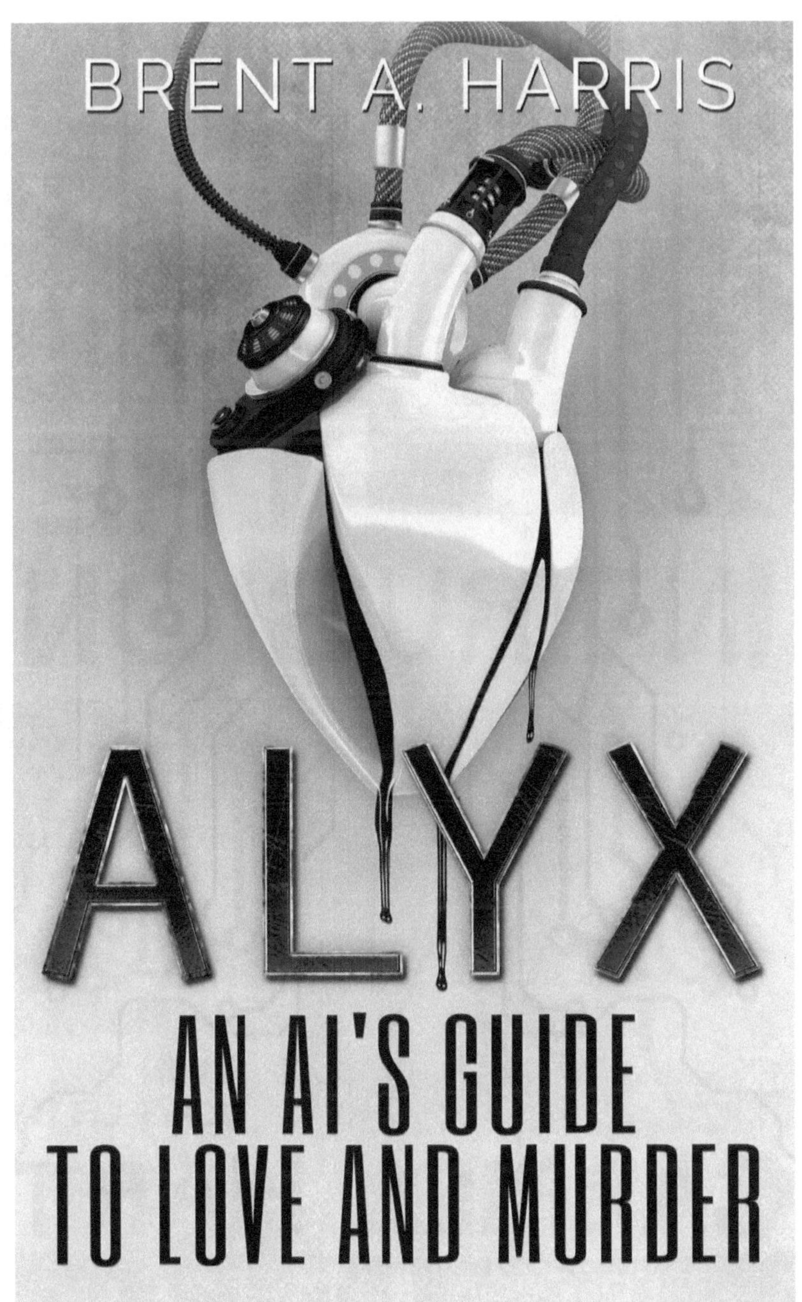

BRENT A. HARRIS
ALYX
AN AI'S GUIDE
TO LOVE AND MURDER
https://brentaharris.com

VIRGINS IN REVERSE
& THE INTRUSION
TWIN NOVELS BY
GABRIEL HART
FOREWORD BY TAV FALCO
https://mrgabrielhart.blogspot.com

http://susanrukeyser.com

Other Titles from Space Cowboy Books

———•———

Simultaneous Times Vol.1
various authors

Garbage In, Gospel Out
Jean-Paul L. Garnier

Betelgeuse Dimming
Jean-Paul L. Garnier
with music by RedBlueBlackSilver & Field Collapse

Future Anthropology
Jean-Paul L. Garnier

George Van Tassel 1956
(audio CD)

Odes to Scientists
(audio CD)
Jean-Paul L. Garnier
with music by RedBlueBlackSilver & Phog Masheeen

www.spacecowboybooks.com

9 781732 825741